MW01702168

ISBN: 978-91-531-3196-0

BJÖRN HÖGDAL

In The Shadows

Author’s Note

When I began writing In The Shadows, I set out to craft a story that wouldn’t just stand apart, it would grip you by the throat and refuse to let go. This isn’t just a tale of terror lurking in the dark; it’s about survival stripped to its core brutal, relentless, and unyielding.

This isn’t a reflection of the past or a journey into introspection. It’s an experience. The characters don’t have time to process the surrounding horrors, and neither will you. There’s no reprieve, no pause to catch your breath. I wanted you, the reader, to feel that same crushing intensity, that same primal drive to push forward when every step feels like the last.

I chose to break away from traditional storytelling norms to make this as raw and real as possible. In a fight for survival, there’s no room for indulgent prose or poetic musings. There’s only action, choices, and their devastating consequences. In The Shadows is chaos personified, throwing you headfirst into an unrelenting storm where every decision carries weight. This is not a story to understand; it’s a story to feel. I hope you find yourself in the thick of it—heart pounding, dread creeping, forced to face the unknown alongside these characters. Draw your own conclusions. Live their terror. And, like them, confront the bitter truth: In this world, nothing is safe. Welcome to the darkness. Stay sharp.

—Björn Högdal

Author’s Warning

In The Shadows is not a story of comfort. It ventures into the darkest depths of survival, human desperation, and unimaginable choices. This narrative contains graphic depictions of violence, loss, and gut-wrenching sacrifice. Innocence is shattered, hope is fleeting, and mercy often comes at the highest price.

Some scenes will disturb. Some will linger. The themes of this story—raw fear, unthinkable decisions, and resilience against the impossible—may leave you questioning more than you’re prepared to answer.

This is a relentless journey, not for the faint of heart.

Reader discretion is strongly advised.

In The Shadows

Prologue

The Birth of The Unknown

The voice emerged from the shadows, heavy with age and burden, recounting truths long buried in blood and fear.

"It began in the bitter heart of winter, the year 1767. Snow fell heavily on the land, muffling the cries of terror that rose from the hills. A small village in Gévaudan was torn apart, its people hunted by something that defied reason. Women and children—snatched from their lives like dying embers—left behind only as grotesque warnings.

At first, they whispered it was wolves. But wolves do not kill with such calculated malice. Rumors spread like a plague, whispering of a beast. A demon. Some called it the wrath of a vengeful spirit. Others claimed it was a curse upon the land itself. Among the survivors—those lucky, or cursed, enough to flee—a name was spoken in trembling tones:

The Ghost of Gévaudan.

They said it was death given form, a shadow that burned red with eyes like blood. Wherever it struck, it left no doubt of its inhumanity. Livestock torn to pieces. Homes desecrated. Hunters vanished, leaving only shredded clothing and pools of darkened blood. Families disappeared into the night, leaving nothing but silence.

Desperate to end the slaughter, the king summoned his greatest warriors—hunters, soldiers, mercenaries—men who had stared into the jaws of death and survived. Our orders were clear: bring it down, no matter the cost.

For days, we tracked it into the heart of the forest, where the air hung thick with decay, and the snow beneath our boots was stained crimson. And then...

It found us.

It came in the dead of night, when even the stars seemed afraid to shine. What we faced was no animal. No earthly predator. It was something born of nightmares—its body cloaked in shadow, its eyes the only light: a searing, malevolent glow. It moved faster than logic could fathom, its strength shattering steel and bone alike. It did not kill for survival.

It killed for the thrill of it.

We fought with everything we had—blades, arrows, fire, fury. The ground turned red as it tore through us like wheat before a scythe. But by some cruel miracle, or curse, we brought it down. As dawn broke, we stood among the dead—our brothers lying still in the snow, the beast's black blood steaming in the cold air.

We thought we had won.

Three days later, the killings began again. Worse this time. Villages burned to the ground. Children ripped from their beds. The truth became clear:

The Ghost of Gévaudan lived.

The king, knowing brute force was not enough, summoned his priests, generals, and advisors. Together, they devised a plan. They chose the best of us—those who had stared into the abyss and walked away alive. Soldiers became something else entirely. We were reforged, trained in secrets, and shaped into weapons.

They called us Phantom.

Our mission was clear: to move unseen, to hunt the darkness before it consumed the light. For years, we waged a silent war, the last shield between humanity and the nightmares it refused to believe in.

But shadows cannot escape the light forever. And now, as crimson eyes burn once more from the depths of the night, the fight begins again.

Phantom must rise.

For the battle was never over. It has only just begun."

The Alpha Awakens

Present Day

Three black stealth helicopters carved silently through the dark sky, racing toward the sprawling, dense forest below. The shadows swallowed them whole, and the rotors' hum dissolved into the heavy fog clinging to the treetops—almost as if the forest itself conspired to bury its secrets.

Inside the lead helicopter, Nathan, the team leader, leaned forward, his voice a controlled growl into the comms. "Satellite images. On-screen. Now." Helmet displays flickered to life, casting ghostly light across the soldiers' grim faces. The campsite was chaos—vehicles twisted and broken, tents reduced to ribbons, the earth strewn with blackened wreckage. It looked like a war zone.

"Why are we here?" a rookie's voice crackled, thin and brittle. "We're hunters, not soldiers."

Nathan's second-in-command chuckled darkly—a sound void of humor. "You don't know what's waiting down there, Aspirant." His tone dropped, cold and final. "Pray you never find out."

Nathan's voice cut through the tension like a blade. "Our objectives are clear: rescue, assess, hunt."

The team echoed in unison, voices steady, drilled into readiness: "Rescue. Assess. Hunt."

The rookie tried again, desperation seeping through. "But what are we hunting? Haven't we seen enough of what they can do?"

Nathan didn't flinch. His words were ice. "If it's what I think it is, you'll be lucky to leave alive. Do your job."

The helicopters banked sharply as the site loomed into view. Nathan barked: "Final equipment check. Helmet cams, night vision, thermal scanners. Weapons hot."

The air in the cabin grew razor-thin, compressed by the weight of readiness. Rifles were loaded. Scanners buzzed to life.

"Deploy MZOs," Nathan ordered. From the trailing choppers, small spherical devices dropped soundlessly. As they landed, faint green beams spread outward, crisscrossing like a luminous spiderweb. Nathan's wrist display lit up—clean readouts, perimeter scanned. He unhooked his line and met the team's waiting eyes. "Let's move."

Nathan landed hard, his boots grinding into gravel stained black with something thicker than water. The air was heavy, damp—tainted.

"You're never this tense," murmured his second-in-command, landing beside him.

Nathan's eyes swept the ground—blood-soaked dirt, streaked crimson in his light. "If it's that thing again…" He exhaled through gritted teeth. "We're in serious trouble."

The team fanned out, moving low and silent, their scanners slicing through the dark. But nothing could have prepared them.

The campsite was carnage. Vehicles ripped open, doors torn clean off their hinges. Metal frames twisted like paper. Blood pooled across the earth, organs and entrails strewn with deliberate malice—like a predator had played with its prey.

"What the hell…" a soldier whispered, his voice breaking. "This isn't an attack. It's a goddamn bloodbath."

Nathan knelt by the tracks carved deep into the mud—impossibly large, unnaturally sharp. His breath stilled. He didn't need confirmation.

"Central," he radioed, voice clipped. "Get me a zoologist. Analyze these prints—"

A nervous voice crackled back. "Based on the pattern and the brutality —"

“I already know,” Nathan interrupted, rising. His face was set like stone. “We’re pulling out. Reinforcements, now.”

Then it came.

The roar.

It didn’t echo—it rolled through the forest like a living thing, vibrating the ground, rattling the bones in their chests. The air itself froze.

“Evacuate!” Nathan thundered. “Move!”

Lines dropped from the hovering helicopters. The team sprinted for extraction as a hulking shadow burst from the treeline.

“GO! GO! GO!” Nathan roared, unleashing silver rounds. The creature shrieked—a sound like metal grinding through flesh—guttural, wrong, and deafening. The bullets hit their mark, but the thing barely slowed.

“Silver?!” the rookie gasped, wide-eyed. “That should’ve killed it!”

Nathan’s jaw tightened, his voice low, haunted. “That just pissed it off. This… is an Alpha.”

The beast retreated, its furious howl reverberating for miles—thick with promise. The last man was pulled aboard, and the choppers lifted, vanishing into the fog.

Nathan stared out the open bay door, his gaze locked on the darkened forest receding below.

“How long have you been tracking it?” his second asked, breath ragged.

“Ten years,” Nathan murmured. His voice carried a weight centuries old. “Our unit’s hunted this thing since 1767.” His words turned colder. “It’s smarter, faster, deadlier than anything you’ve ever faced.”

The helicopter climbed, the reserve swallowed by mist and shadow. Nathan’s whisper lingered in the dark.

“And this fight… it’s just beginning.”

24 Hours Later

The television screen flickered to life. A news anchor sat stiffly at her desk, illuminated by the harsh glow of emergency lights. Behind her, the reserve was a sea of fog, pulsing red and blue.

"Breaking news from southern Alaska," she began, her voice taut. "Twenty-five bodies have been recovered under what authorities describe as… 'highly unusual circumstances.' No survivors."

The screen flickered—static fractured the feed. The camera cut to helicopters rising through the mist, black body bags swaying beneath them.

"What could have been so extreme," the anchor pressed, her voice trembling, "that it required the involvement of a covert government unit?"

Handheld footage flashed: soldiers clad in black, sweeping through the reserve with weapons drawn. Their faces were obscured.

"Families demand answers," the anchor continued, leaning forward, her voice cracking. "But officials remain silent. What happened in those woods? And why can't we know?"

The broadcast fractured into static, then blackness. A beat of silence. Then, words etched in stark white:

"What was lost… has awakened."

The Fence

The broadcast glowed from Sarah's phone, the screen's faint light cutting sharp shadows across her face in the pitch-dark of her parked car. Outside, the world was cloaked in fog, dense and silent, as though the reserve itself was holding its breath.

Sarah's Thoughts: Twenty-five dead. No survivors. And they're hiding something. I have to see it for myself.

She turned off the broadcast, the sudden silence heavy, and leaned back in her seat. The cold air bit at her lungs, her breath misting the windshield. Beyond the fogged glass, the drizzle tapped an uneven rhythm on the car roof, hypnotic in its dissonance.

From far off, the faint thrum of helicopter rotors carried through the night—low and steady. Soldiers' voices drifted, distorted by the distance and swallowed by the thick mist. Sarah shivered. They were closer than she'd hoped.

Her phone buzzed, breaking the trance. She snatched it up, her heart jumping.

Voice on the Phone: "Sarah, you need to be careful." The voice was sharp, urgent, each word pressed and clipped. "They have eyes everywhere."

The line went dead.

Sarah's gaze darted across the empty road. The fog curled like phantom tendrils through the skeletal trees, shifting as though it had a life of its own. The chill sank deeper into her bones, heavier now—oppressive.

Pulling her jacket tighter, she grabbed her camera and slipped her recorder into her pocket, double-checking both. The metal of the camera strap felt ice-cold against her fingers. She slid out of the car, quiet as a shadow, her breath clouding instantly in the freezing air.

The distant hum of generators blended with the murmur of unseen voices. Overhead, the faint drumbeat of helicopters pressed against her ears, vibrating the stillness. Sarah crouched low and moved toward the fence, each step deliberate, each crunch of gravel a risk.

Sarah's Thoughts: What are they hiding in there?

The floodlights struck through the fog like knives, cutting long, jagged shadows into the underbrush. Sarah pressed herself against a thicket of bushes, the branches clawing at her jacket as she peered out.

Beyond the fence, it looked like another world. Dark figures moved with practiced efficiency—men in heavy armor, faceless behind their helmets. Unmarked vehicles sat idle, their engines rumbling softly, and looming above them was a strange container being loaded onto a truck. Sarah zoomed her camera lens, her finger trembling against the shutter.

Click.

The sound was deafening in her ears. She froze, heart pounding. No one seemed to notice.

She adjusted the lens again, focusing on a marking on the truck's door—a strange symbol. It looked old, almost archaic: a snarling wolf's head above two crossed swords. The sight of it sent a chill crawling up her spine, her pulse quickening.

Sarah's Thoughts: What does that symbol mean?

Her camera clicked softly again. She took more shots—close-ups of the container, the symbol, the men.

Then she heard it.

Snap.

A branch breaking.

Sarah's breath hitched as two guards' flashlights flicked toward the sound. The beams sliced through the fog like blades of light.

Guard 1: "Did you hear that?"

Guard 2: "Could be an animal. But let's check it out."

Their boots crunched against gravel as they moved forward, the lights sweeping through the trees—closer, closer. Sarah flattened herself against the cold earth, willing herself invisible. Her chest burned as she held her breath, her hands trembling around the camera.

The beams of light crept closer.

Sarah's Thoughts: Don't move. Don't breathe. Just a little longer…

The guards were almost on top of her. The sound of their voices felt suffocating. Sarah's fingers curled into the dirt, panic rising in her throat.

Then, a crash.

Something loud—a metallic clang—echoed from the far side of the clearing. The guards froze, their flashlights jerking toward the noise.

Guard 1: "Over there!"

Guard 2: "Move!"

The guards turned and sprinted toward the sound, their voices fading into the fog.

Sarah exhaled a shaky breath, her heart slamming against her ribs. She didn't wait. Staying low, she crept back, step by step, her body trembling with adrenaline. When she was far enough, she bolted.

Branches clawed at her clothes as she ran, her pulse a frantic drumbeat in her ears. She didn't stop until she reached her car, throwing herself inside. Her hands shook as she fumbled with the keys, her breath ragged.

The engine roared to life, and she peeled away, gravel spitting beneath her tires.

Sarah's Thoughts: That was too close. But I got what I needed.

She drove through the mist-soaked darkness, her mind racing with what she'd seen. The images burned behind her eyes—men in armor, the strange container, and that symbol.

As the fog swallowed the road behind her, a cold truth gnawed at the edge of her thoughts: whatever was happening in that reserve, it was bigger—and far darker—than she'd imagined.

And now, she was part of it. As she drove back to her cabin, the images she captured replayed over and over in her mind. Something was terribly wrong in that reserve, and now, she was part of it.

The night clung to her like the fog outside, oppressive and thick. As she pulled into her driveway, the unsettling quiet felt sharper, almost alive. She hurried inside, locking the door behind her, her breath shallow.

Sarah's Search at the Archive

The morning sun sliced through the dense canopy of trees, casting slanted beams of golden light that danced across the forest floor. Sarah stepped out of her cabin, the crisp, cool air biting at her skin, filling her lungs with a sharp freshness that felt almost foreign. The world seemed suspended in the stillness of the early morning, the quiet hum of the woods surrounding her, yet her mind buzzed relentlessly with the memory of last night—the heaviness of the unknown, the pulse of dread, and the undercurrent of excitement. Today, she was determined to find answers—answers that had eluded her for far too long.

Her eyes flicked toward the car parked a few meters away, its metallic surface gleaming in the low sunlight. The gravel crunched beneath her boots as she moved towards it, the weight of the decision pressing down on her. The village, just a fifteen-minute drive, felt miles away. The winding roads, the thick forest—everything about it had an isolated, almost forgotten feel, like the kind of place time had neglected to touch.

She fumbled with her keys, deciding that driving would be quicker, less conspicuous, than walking the narrow, often deserted paths. She turned the key, and the engine roared to life, the sound momentarily filling the silence.

The tires of her car crunched over the gravel, a steady rhythm that seemed to echo through the trees. Yet, despite the sound, a creeping unease coiled in Sarah's stomach. The trees loomed around her like dark sentinels, their branches swaying with a faint creak in the morning breeze. She glanced at the rearview mirror more than once, half-expecting to see something—someone—lurking in the shadows behind her. But the mirror only reflected the trees, their shadows stretching long and ominous. Still, that feeling—of being watched—clung to her, persistent and cold, like a second skin.

The village emerged slowly from the trees, a cluster of quaint houses with steep roofs and well-tended gardens. It was picturesque, almost too perfect, as if it were preserved in a bubble of time. The air smelled faintly of damp earth and flowers, the scent of a place untouched by the modern world. Sarah turned onto the main street, passing a few locals. They stood in front of a small café, exchanging quiet words, their eyes flicking up at her car as it passed. Their gazes followed her, sharp and guarded, as if they knew she didn't belong.

She parked in front of the local archive, a weathered stone building standing in quiet defiance against the passage of time. Ivy clung to its walls like a veil, and the arched windows reflected the morning sun in eerie, fractured patterns. The faint scent of musty wood and old paper drifted in the air as Sarah stepped out of her car. It was the kind of place that should have felt inviting, yet an unsettling chill ran down her spine as her feet touched the ground. Something darker lingered here, a silent tension in the air, just beneath the surface, like a storm waiting to break.

The bell above the door jingled as Sarah stepped inside, the sound sharp in the quiet of the room. The air was thick with the scent of old books and dust, the smell of forgotten memories. Soft lamps cast long, distorted shadows that stretched across the shelves, giving the room an almost surreal feel. Each step she took on the creaky hardwood floor seemed to echo through the silence.

An elderly woman sat behind the desk, her eyes sharp and calculating as they fixed on Sarah the moment she entered. Her gaze lingered, assessing, before she gave a curt nod.

"Good morning," Sarah said, forcing a polite smile, though her voice betrayed the unease swirling in her chest. "I'm looking for information on the local history—specifically about the wildlife reserve."

The woman hesitated, her sharp eyes narrowing as if weighing Sarah's words. She nodded slowly, almost reluctantly. "We have some records. Not many, but you're welcome to look." Her voice dropped to a whisper as she added, "All the rangers were evacuated—immediate orders. Whatever's happening out there, it's serious."

A chill washed over Sarah. "Evacuated? Why?"

The woman shook her head, her lips pressed together in a tight line. "They didn't tell us. Just packed up and left. Haven't seen anything like it before."

The words hung in the air, heavy with meaning, and Sarah's heart skipped a beat. There was something wrong—something that gnawed at her insides, twisting tighter with each passing second. She thanked the woman and stepped deeper into the archive, the wood beneath her feet creaking with every step, as if the building itself was watching her.

At the back of the room, she found a small table, cluttered with stacks of old papers and dusty files. The faint scent of mildew hung in the air as she began to sift through them. Most of the articles were mundane—reports of town meetings, local events, the occasional mention of a lost hiker. But as Sarah dug deeper, she began to notice something troubling. Every few years, there was a brief mention of a disappearance or a strange sighting in the woods, always followed by a curt statement that the case had been closed, with no further investigation.

Her fingers trembled as she scribbled down dates and details in her notebook, her heart racing. The pieces were starting to come together, forming a pattern too consistent to be ignored. It was as if someone—or something—had been trying to erase these events from history, to bury the truth beneath layers of dust and time.

As she reached for another stack of papers, something caught her eye. A thick, dusty tome sat on one of the nearby shelves, its leather cover cracked and worn. The title, barely visible, gleamed in faded gold: *The Beast of Gévaudan*. The book seemed to pulse with a strange energy, an unspoken invitation. Sarah felt an inexplicable pull as her fingers brushed against its surface. She pulled it from the shelf, the weight of it surprising, like the burden of history itself.

She flipped open the cover, the pages brittle and fragile, the scent of old paper mixing with the musty air around her. The first few chapters detailed the legendary tale—the monstrous wolf-like creature that terrorized the French countryside in the 18th century. But as she turned the pages, something caught her attention—drawings, notes, and sketches scrawled in the margins in a hurried, frantic hand. The beast was depicted in monstrous detail, towering over terrified villagers, but there were also strange symbols, symbols she had never seen before, etched alongside it.

Her breath caught in her throat when she turned to a page near the middle of the book. There, etched in painstaking detail, was a symbol—the same symbol she had seen on the side of the truck the night before. Her pulse quickened as she traced the lines with her fingers, a chill racing down her spine.

"What does it mean?" she whispered, the words barely escaping her lips. The world seemed to slow as her mind raced, piecing together fragments of a story much darker than she could have imagined.

She didn't hear the soft creak of the floorboards behind her. She didn't feel the presence until it was almost too late. The air shifted, thickening with a cold, oppressive weight. She froze, her muscles locking in place as she felt eyes upon her—cold, unyielding eyes.

"Finding what you're looking for?" The voice was low, smooth, and unfamiliar, its tone sending a shiver up her spine.

Sarah turned slowly, her heart hammering in her chest, to find a man standing behind her. His dark suit was perfectly pressed, his gaze unwavering and piercing, as if he could see straight through her. Every inch of him radiated danger.

"I—yes, I was just… doing some research," Sarah stammered, her voice barely a whisper as her hands trembled, closing the book. "About local legends."

The man's gaze flicked briefly to the book before returning to her. He didn't speak at first, just studied her, his eyes narrowing slightly, as if weighing her very soul. Then, with a subtle nod, he took a step back.

"Be careful what you dig up," he said softly, a note of warning in his voice. “Some stories are best left buried.”

Without another word, he turned and walked away, his footsteps eerily silent against the creaking floorboards. Sarah sat frozen, the words echoing in her mind, a cold sweat clinging to her skin. She waited, straining for any sound, but the library was still—utterly still.

Taking a deep breath, she gathered the strength to stand. The book felt heavy in her hands, its weight an anchor to a truth she wasn’t sure she was ready to face. She had to leave, had to figure out what it all meant. But as she made her way to the door, the oppressive feeling of being watched crept up again. The shadows in the corners of the room felt darker, deeper, like they were hiding more than just forgotten memories.

With one last glance at the silent library, she pushed open the door. The air outside was sharp and cold, the quiet village more unsettling than ever. She hurried to her car, her pulse racing in her ears, the world around her seeming quieter, emptier.

As she climbed into the car, she glanced back at the building, half-expecting to see the man watching her from one of the windows. But there was nothing—only the dark shapes of the bookshelves beyond the glass.

She started the car, the engine purring to life, and drove away, her mind spinning with everything she had uncovered. Too many coincidences, too many connections. Whatever was happening in the reserve, it was tied to something much older, much darker than she could have imagined.

The drive back to the cabin was uneventful, but Sarah couldn't shake the unease that had settled over her. The sun, struggling to stay above the treetops, cast long, spindly shadows that seemed to stretch and reach like fingers across the forest floor. As she neared her cabin, the light seemed to weaken, the shadows growing bolder, more sinister.

She pulled up to her cabin, the once-familiar place now feeling alien, as if the very air had thickened. The sun, low in the sky, seemed to battle the looming trees, casting eerie, ghostly shapes that danced along the ground and walls. It was as though the woods themselves were alive, watching her every move.

Sarah hurried inside, the sensation of being followed growing unbearable. She slammed the door shut behind her, the sound echoing through the empty cabin. The warmth inside felt suddenly stifling, and she leaned against the door, eyes darting to the window as though expecting someone to be there. But there was nothing—just the creeping shadows outside, moving slowly in the dying light.

Into the Darkness

Sarah sat in her small cabin, the dim glow from her laptop the only light in the room. The screen displayed a collage of images: the ominous insignia from the military vehicle, maps of the wildlife reserve, and files documenting unexplained disappearances. Her gaze locked onto the emblem—a snarling wolf's head flanked by crossed swords.

It emanated an aura of authority and danger, as though it carried the weight of something primal, something ancient. Yet here it was, firmly rooted in the present, worn by soldiers operating in secrecy. A mix of fascination and unease churned within her as she studied it.

Turning to The Beast of Gévaudan, Sarah carefully flipped through its brittle pages. Her hands trembled slightly as she scanned the text until, halfway through, she found it: a hand-drawn replica of the very same symbol.

The wolf's head, ferocious and predatory, stared back at her. Beneath it, two swords crossed defiantly. Below the illustration, faded French words read:

"Les chasseurs de l'ombre. Nous portons l'épée pour faire vadra la lumière." (The hunters of the shadows. We carry the sword to bring light.)

Sarah's Thoughts: This isn't a coincidence. These people… they've been here for centuries.

Her pulse quickened as she read on. The crumbling paper revealed detailed accounts of soldiers pursuing a beast—vast, intelligent, and seemingly unstoppable. Yellowed illustrations showed men clad in armor, bearing the same emblem, standing victorious over a creature that defied description.

A shiver traced her spine as her eyes fell upon one particular sketch: a monstrous figure with glowing eyes, surrounded by chaos and terror. The artist's hand had captured something deeply unsettling, something Sarah couldn't tear her gaze from. Those eyes—they felt alive, almost as if watching her through the faded ink.

Sarah's Thoughts: If something like this existed… what's lurking in the reserve now?

Her notebook lay open beside her, filled with cases she had meticulously documented over five years. Each death followed a harrowing pattern—no survivors, bodies torn apart in ways that no known animal could explain. Beside each entry, she had written the same note: Covered up.

The silence in the cabin was suffocating, broken only by the steady tick of the clock. Sarah hesitated, then picked up her phone and dialed a familiar number.

Sarah: "Hey, it's me. I need to ask you something… Do you recognize this symbol?"

She sent the photo.

A long pause followed, heavy and tense. Finally, the voice on the other end exhaled.

Contact: "Sarah, I warned you to stop. That symbol… it belongs to more than just a military unit. They're hunters. They deal with things that shouldn't exist."

Sarah: voice trembling "What things?"

Contact: lowering their voice "Creatures, Sarah. Beasts like the one in that book. They're real. And if they're involved… you're in way over your head."

Sarah's breath caught as she flipped back to a sketch in the book: a soldier towering over a slain beast, its glowing eyes eerily alive even in death.

Sarah: “I can’t walk away. People are dying. I need to understand what’s going on.”

Contact: frustrated “You’re not listening. If you keep digging, they’ll come for you. You need to disappear before they make you disappear.”

The line went dead. Sarah stared at her phone, her hands trembling. The room seemed smaller now, the shadows heavier.

Turning back to her laptop, Sarah plunged into her research, the glow of the screen her only light. Hours blurred together, and frustration mounted as every lead turned into a dead end. Then, she stumbled upon an old forum post. A user claimed to have seen the same emblem at the site of an “animal attack” across the country.

Sarah’s Thoughts: This isn’t just happening here.

Her fingers flew over the keyboard as she typed a message. No response. Her frustration grew as she scrolled through more threads, vague mentions of cover-ups and conspiracies filling the screen. Just as she was about to close her laptop, a notification blinked.

Anonymous User: “You’re looking in the wrong places. Want answers? Find John Goldman.”

Her breath caught. That name! She typed a response, but the user logged out before she could hit send.

Sarah’s Thoughts: There’s no turning back now.

As the night deepened, Sarah called contact after contact, desperately seeking information about John Goldman. Finally, she got a lead—a nurse at a care facility outside the city. She jotted down the address, her heart pounding.

Sarah’s Thoughts: If anyone knows what’s going on, it’s him.

Stretching stiff muscles, she glanced out the window. The darkness pressed against the glass like a living thing, and the clock showed it was past midnight.

With a sigh, Sarah began packing for the next day—her notes, camera, and phone. Each movement felt deliberate, as though the weight of her discovery bore down on her.

Sarah's Thoughts: I have to do this. I have to find the truth.

As she zipped her bag shut, a faint creak broke the silence. Her body froze.

Snap.

The sound of a branch cracking echoed through the stillness.

Moving cautiously to the window, her heart hammered as she peered into the night. The faint moonlight barely pierced the thick shadows. She saw nothing, but the feeling was undeniable.

Something was out there. Watching. Waiting.

Sarah turned from the window, her resolve hardening. Whatever was outside wouldn't stop her. She'd find John Goldman. No matter what it took.

Shadows of Secrets

The next morning, just at dawn, she gets into her car. The air is thick with the lingering chill of the early hours, and she pulls her jacket tighter around herself as she starts the engine. The cabin area is still and quiet, the only sound the low hum of the forest.

Sarah's Thoughts: This is my chance. I have to be careful.

She drives slowly through the small town, which is barely awake. A few streetlights cast long shadows over the narrow roads, and an ominous stillness hangs over the place. Sarah passes the bookstore she visited earlier, and her eyes catch on the window display. The old book is still there, with its dark, captivating story.

Sarah's Thoughts: There's something about that book… something I need to understand.

She doesn't stop this time, but her mind is filled with questions and unanswered clues. With steady hands on the wheel, she drives on, out of the town and toward the nursing home. As the sun slowly rises over the horizon, she feels that a new day brings both answers and dangers. She knows this might be the most dangerous journey she's ever undertaken.

Sarah's Thoughts: John Goldman… I hope you have the answers I need.

Sarah drives out of the small town, watching as the sun begins to climb beautifully over the treetops. Her thoughts whirl around the questions she still doesn't have answers to.

What does John Goldman have to do with all of this? And who sent that anonymous message?

She shakes her head, trying to focus on the road ahead. Her GPS directs her to turn off the main road onto a smaller gravel path. The trees on either side grow dense, closing in like a tunnel as the dirt road crunches beneath her tires. Every bump, every noise from the car makes her pulse quicken. The forest feels oppressive here, almost too quiet. No wind. No birds. Just her thoughts and the steady rumble of the tires on gravel.

Soon, she reaches a tall chain-link fence. The gate stands open, but the level of security is hard to miss. Cameras, barbed wire. The place exudes an unsettling atmosphere. The gravel gives way to smooth asphalt, and the road feels more like the entrance to a prison than a nursing home.

Why so much security in such a remote place?

Sarah's thoughts darken as she pulls into the empty parking lot. Only one other car is there, sitting eerily alone. She parks next to it and exhales deeply before turning off the engine. Something feels off, she thinks as she scans her surroundings. Despite the sun having now fully risen over the treetops, casting a soft glow across the open field that surrounds the nursing home, there's an undeniable sense of isolation.

The building itself looks modern, almost too sleek for being out here in the middle of nowhere. Sarah double-checks her belongings—

camera, notes, phone. But just as she's about to open the car door, there's a sudden knock on her window. She jumps, her heart racing.

A man stands outside, looking at her with a measured, assessing gaze. She opens the door slowly, her hands trembling slightly as she grips the handle.

"Sarah?" the man asks.

Her pulse quickens again. This isn't the deep, warning voice from the archive call. This man is younger, maybe in his early thirties. His posture isn't that of an office worker; there's a quiet strength to him, his broad shoulders and confident stance suggesting he's been in more dangerous situations than she can imagine.

She exhales. "Yes, I'm Sarah," she says, her voice a little shaky.

The man extends his hand. "Nathan Ward," he introduces himself. His handshake is firm, almost too firm, and Sarah's nerves buzz. He's no ordinary staff member, she realizes.

Why does this feel so wrong? she wonders, the unease settling deeper in her chest.

Stepping out of the car, she follows Nathan as he gestures toward the entrance. Every step feels like she's being pulled further into something dangerous. As they walk, she studies him from the corner of her eye. His profile is sharp, his jaw clenched as if he's suppressing something. There's a hardness in his expression, a tension in his movements, like someone who's seen far too much.

Sarah can't shake the feeling. What is someone like him doing at a nursing home?

"Have you met John Goldman before?" Sarah asks, her voice tentative, searching for more information.

Nathan stops just before they reach the front doors, his gaze sliding sideways to meet hers. There's a weight in his eyes, something unspoken but heavy with meaning. "Not exactly," he replies, his tone careful. "But I've heard enough about him. You'll understand when you meet him." His words, though vague, are laced with significance, like he's holding back something important.

A shiver runs through her. What exactly am I walking into?

As they step inside the nursing home, the modern interior does nothing to calm her nerves. The sleekness of the place contrasts sharply with the eerie emptiness around them. The air feels thick, like the silence is watching them.

Nathan led her through the silent, empty corridors, each step echoing in the sterile environment. The place was too clean, too modern—nothing like the rundown nursing homes she had imagined. The polished surfaces and silence only deepened the unease gnawing at her stomach.

As they reached the end of the hallway, Nathan motioned for Sarah to wait while he spoke to John. His expression didn't invite questions, so she simply nodded and watched as he disappeared into the room, the door closing with a soft click behind him. Sarah stood awkwardly for a moment, unsure of where to go. The sleek, sterile environment around her didn't help the rising discomfort gnawing at her chest. She spotted a chair nearby and sat down, her eyes darting to the wall clock as the seconds ticked by slowly.

Hospitals. Nursing homes. She hated them. The cold, impersonal air. The muted, lifeless colors. They were reminders of things long buried in her past, things she tried not to think about.

Her stomach twisted as the memories crept back. Years ago, sitting in a hospital room, the beeping machines, the smell of disinfectant clinging to her clothes. Her mother had been so frail, so quiet, and no matter how hard Sarah had tried to be strong, that helplessness had consumed her. It was the feeling that no matter what she did, she couldn't fight what was coming.

The waiting now felt much the same. Like an eternity stretched into minutes. The muffled sounds of conversation behind the closed door only heightened the tension. She shifted uncomfortably in her seat, her fingers playing with the strap of her bag.

Her eyes drifted across the cold, sterile environment. Her discomfort was palpable. Hospitals. Nursing homes. They had always unsettled her. The clinical smell, the unnatural quiet—it all brought back memories she preferred to keep buried.

She shifted in her seat, trying to ignore the slow ticking of the wall clock. It reminded her too much of those long, agonizing hours by her mother's bedside, waiting for the inevitable. The feeling of helplessness crept back, gnawing at her as she waited to meet John. This was no different. The same sense of dread, the same knowledge that something terrible had already taken place, and there was nothing she could do to stop it.

As she sat there, her gaze was drawn to the far corner of the room. It was subtle, almost hidden in the shadows, but a cabinet stood there—sleek, metallic, with a small digital keypad on the front. The bright red digits glowed in the dim light of the hallway.

Her breath hitched. Why would a nursing home need something like that? The thought of it gnawed at her. It was out of place in a facility like this, where everything else screamed quiet serenity, or at least tried to. She frowned, her mind racing. What could be so important that it needed to be locked away behind a code?

Sarah's instincts kicked in. She couldn't shake the feeling that whatever was in that cabinet was tied to everything she'd been investigating. The military presence at the reserve, the strange symbols, the secrecy—it all felt connected somehow. She had learned to trust her gut, and right now, it was screaming at her that something was wrong.

She stole another glance at the closed door, behind which Nathan was speaking to John. The conversation was muffled, distant. Her fingers itched to do something—to act—but what could she do? Nathan had made it clear that this place wasn't what it seemed. And yet, here she was, sitting in a waiting room that felt more like a stage, while the real action was happening just out of sight.

Her eyes flicked back to the cabinet. She knew she shouldn't, but the temptation to get up and inspect it was almost overwhelming. What could be so secret, locked away in a nursing home of all places?

Just then, the door creaked open behind her. Sarah jumped, quickly pulling her gaze away from the cabinet. Nathan stepped out, his face as unreadable as before. He nodded toward her.

"John is ready to see you now."

Sarah hesitated for a moment before standing up, her body stiff from the tension of waiting. As she rose from the chair, her eyes couldn't help but drift back to the cabinet. That glowing keypad—it almost felt like it was daring her to uncover what was hidden inside. The thought sent a chill down her spine.

Just as she turned her gaze back to Nathan, she saw it—a flicker of understanding in his eyes. His expression remained calm, but the way his gaze briefly darted to the cabinet told her everything she needed to know.

He knows.

Nathan didn't say a word, but his jaw tightened slightly, and for a fraction of a second, the air between them grew heavier. Sarah felt her pulse quicken, her curiosity now mingling with a sharp sense of caution. Whatever was locked away in that cabinet, Nathan was aware of its significance—and he didn't want her anywhere near it.

"John is ready for you," Nathan said, his tone controlled, as if nothing had happened. But the way he subtly positioned himself between her and the cabinet as he gestured toward the door wasn't lost on her. It was a quiet warning.

Sarah nodded, trying to keep her expression calm, but as she turned toward John's room, she felt the weight of Nathan's eyes on her back. Whatever was locked inside that cabinet, she knew she'd have to find out—eventually. But not right now.

She stepped through the doorway, her thoughts swirling, and prepared herself to meet John.

Meeting John

As Sarah stepped into the room, she immediately sensed something was off. It wasn't the sterile, impersonal space she had expected from a nursing home. The room felt too personalized, too settled, like a small apartment rather than a temporary recovery space.

A narrow bed sat against the wall, and beside it was a small table with two wooden chairs. A vase of fresh flowers stood in the center, and on the bedside table, a framed photograph caught her eye. In the photo, John looked younger, standing beside a woman and two children, all smiling brightly. It was a simple family portrait, but the happy expressions felt frozen, like they belonged to another time—before everything had changed.

Her gaze moved across the room. A dresser with a mirror stood against one wall, and a television was mounted above it. The large window offered a stunning view of the field and the forest beyond, sunlight pouring through the glass, casting a soft glow over the space. Despite the warmth, the room felt unsettling. It wasn't just the scars that marred John's appearance—it was the eerie stillness of the room, like it was suspended in time.

Sarah's stomach tightened as she realized how out of place the room felt. This wasn't a place for recovery. It was a place where someone had been left to wait.

Her breath hitched as she noticed John standing by the window, his back to her, hands clasped behind him. Though he hadn't turned to acknowledge her, she knew he was aware of her presence.

For a moment, the silence pressed down on her, heavy and suffocating. Her eyes drifted back to the photograph by the bed, her heart twisting at the sight of the smiling family. Whoever they were, they felt like ghosts of a life long gone.

John finally moved. Slowly, deliberately, he turned from the window to face her. His face was crisscrossed with deep scars—jagged lines that ran down from his temple to his jaw. His arms, visible beneath his rolled-up sleeves, bore similar marks, like battle wounds etched into his skin. The sight made Sarah freeze, a cold shiver running through her. What had this man been through?

"Sarah, I presume," John said, his voice rough and gravelly. His tone carried no surprise, only a resigned calm, as if he had been expecting her for a long time.

Sarah nodded, her throat tight. "Yes," she managed to say, her voice barely above a whisper. Her eyes kept drifting to the scars, the deep lines that seemed to tell a story she couldn't yet grasp.

John noticed her gaze and let out a low chuckle, though it held no humor. "Wondering what happened to me?" he asked, his tone casual but distant. "Everyone does."

Sarah's heart skipped a beat. "I—no, I mean…" She trailed off, unsure of what to say.

John waved it off with a slight shake of his head. "Doesn't matter," he muttered, turning back toward the window. His voice grew softer, more detached. "Not anymore. Now it's just… waiting."

"Waiting?" Sarah repeated, frowning. Something about the way he said the word made her uneasy. The room, the photo, the quiet—it all felt wrong. "Waiting for what?"

John didn't respond right away. His gaze stayed fixed on the forest outside the window, as though he saw something out there she couldn't. "For whatever comes next," he finally said, his voice barely more than a whisper.

Nathan moved silently, taking the chair by the bed with an air of calm authority. The slight creak of the wooden legs echoed in the quiet room as he settled into his seat. Sarah felt her breath catch as the air in the room seemed to thicken, the smell of old wood and faint antiseptic lingering. There was something clinical about the space, yet lived-in—an odd blend of fresh flowers from the vase and the sterile scent that clung to the walls like a ghost.

John, standing by the window, barely moved. His back remained toward her, but she caught the briefest flicker of his eyes as he cast a quick, assessing glance at Nathan, then at her. The expression was fleeting, but the weight of it hung in the air. When his gaze returned to the window, it was as though he was absorbing the world outside, letting it wash over him like a shield.

"I see you've met Nathan," John said, his voice gravelly, as if every word had to scrape its way out of him. There was no warmth in his tone—just something flat, resigned. His profile, with its deeply etched lines and scars, seemed hard, weathered by whatever had happened in his past.

Sarah's heart beat a little faster. She stole a glance at Nathan. He sat perfectly still, hands resting on his knees, his face a mask of calm control. The intensity of his silence felt like a presence all on its own. Sarah's gaze darted between the two men, trying to make sense of the dynamic in the room. Why did it feel like Nathan was in charge, even though he hadn't spoken?

The weight of John's words made her stomach churn. "Whatever happens during this talk," he continued, his voice heavy, like it carried a burden too great to share, "whatever Nathan says, we must follow."

Sarah blinked, her pulse quickening. Her brow furrowed slightly, a flicker of confusion and unease crossing her face. Her throat felt tight as she glanced back at Nathan, who remained unmoving, his expression unreadable. His gaze, cold and steady, flicked briefly toward her, almost as if measuring her reaction. There was no hint of reassurance in his face—just a quiet, calculated stillness.

What did John mean? Why was Nathan the one to follow? Her mind raced, trying to piece together the situation. There was something unspoken here, something deeply unsettling that she wasn't privy to.

The faint rustle of fabric drew her attention back to John, who had shifted slightly, still staring out the window. He let out a heavy sigh, his broad shoulders sinking as though the weight of his words had finally settled. "It's for our safety," he added quietly, his voice barely more than a whisper.

The words sent a chill down Sarah's spine. For our safety. The room suddenly felt too small, too confined, despite the open window and the vastness of the view outside. The scent of fresh flowers mingled with the lingering traces of antiseptic, making her head spin. She had walked into this room expecting answers, but now she was left with more questions, the atmosphere thick with unspoken rules and hidden dangers.

John's expression remained distant, his scarred face turned back toward the forest as if it held all the answers he couldn't give. His jaw clenched slightly, the lines on his face deepening with whatever thoughts were churning behind his eyes. His fingers twitched against the windowsill, betraying a tension he didn't allow to fully surface.

Sarah swallowed hard, her gaze drifting once again to Nathan. He hadn't moved, his posture rigid, but his eyes were sharp, tracking her every subtle movement. There was a quiet authority in him, a restraint that spoke of experience. She couldn't shake the feeling that, despite his calm exterior, Nathan was prepared for something she couldn't yet see.

Sarah's thoughts spiraled as she sat between these two men, both of whom seemed to know more than they were letting on. Nathan's silence, John's cryptic words—it all felt like part of a bigger, darker puzzle. Her stomach knotted as she tried to make sense of it.

The seconds dragged on, the room filled with a palpable tension. Sarah's palms were slick with sweat, her fingers curling slightly in her lap as she resisted the urge to ask the burning questions swirling in her mind. What had she walked into? And why did it feel like, despite being the one asking questions, she was already in too deep?

The Past Unfolds

The quiet tension in John's room hung like a dense fog, but Sarah's determination refused to waver. John's words replayed in her mind: "We need to start from the beginning." This wasn't just a story he was about to tell; it was a reckoning.

John leaned forward, resting his scarred hands on his knees. His gaze dropped, and the weight of what he was about to say seemed to sink into his very being. Nathan, ever the silent observer, shifted slightly in his seat but said nothing. His presence was both reassuring and unnerving, as if he alone knew the full extent of what was coming.

"Fairbanks, Alaska," John began, his gravelly voice soft but resolute. "That's where it all started. My family—Emily, Lucas, Erika, and little Jacob. We had a good life. I thought we were untouchable."

Sarah's pen moved quickly across her notebook, her gaze darting between John and Nathan. She could feel the story tightening its grip on her.

"It was supposed to be an adventure," John continued. "Our first real vacation together. I rented a camper, planned everything—the trails, the campgrounds. It was perfect, or so I thought. We left with so much excitement, so much… innocence."

His voice faltered, and his hand moved to the photograph he had shown Sarah earlier. He traced the faces in the picture—his wife, his children—as though grounding himself.

"The first few days were magical," he said, a faint, bitter smile tugging at his lips. "Lucas loved the stars. He'd stay up late, pointing out constellations to Erika. Emily would laugh and tell him to go to bed, but I'd let him stay up just a little longer. And Jacob… Jacob was just a baby, always giggling at every little thing."

John's smile faded, replaced by a shadow of pain. "But then we reached the reserve. That's when it all started to unravel."

Sarah's hand stilled for a moment, the pen poised above the paper. "The reserve?" she asked, her voice barely above a whisper.

John nodded, his gaze darkening. "It was beautiful—too beautiful. Towering trees, crystal-clear streams, the kind of place you see in postcards. But the silence… the silence was wrong. No birds. No rustling leaves. Just this… oppressive stillness."

Nathan's eyes flicked toward John, his expression unreadable. Sarah noticed the subtle exchange but focused on John as he continued.

"The first night, I thought it was just the kids' excitement keeping me up. But then I heard it. Scratching, pacing, just outside the camper. I told myself it was an animal, maybe a bear. But the tracks… they weren't normal."

He paused, his voice tightening with emotion. "The tracks were massive. Too large for any wolf or bear. And the claws… they looked like… fingers."

Sarah’s stomach churned. She could feel the fear creeping into the room, wrapping itself around them.

“I didn’t tell Emily,” John said, his voice breaking slightly. “She was so happy. The kids were happy. I couldn’t… I couldn’t ruin it. So I stayed up that night, watching, waiting. And then… it came.”

The room seemed to grow colder. John’s gaze lifted to meet Sarah’s, and for the first time, she saw the raw terror in his eyes.

“It wasn’t an animal,” he said, his voice barely above a whisper. “It was something else—something intelligent. It circled the camper, testing us, taunting us. And when it attacked…”

John’s hands trembled, and Nathan leaned forward slightly, his eyes sharp. “John,” Nathan said quietly, his voice steady, “you don’t have to relive this.”

John shook his head, his jaw tightening. “No. She needs to know. They need to know.”

He turned back to Sarah, his voice stronger now. “It tore through the walls like paper,” John said, his voice trembling. “Lucas… he ran. Into the woods. I told him to keep running, to not look back. But Emily, Erika, and Jacob…” He faltered, his hands gripping the edge of the chair so tightly his knuckles turned white. “They were trapped in the camper. I could hear them screaming, calling for me to help, but I couldn’t reach them. Their voices… they still haunt me.”

Sarah’s chest tightened, her eyes stinging with unshed tears. She could feel the weight of John's loss, the unbearable pain he carried.

"I fought it," John said, his voice raw. "I tried. But it was unstoppable. It didn't just kill—it destroyed. It… played with us. Like we were nothing."

The room fell into a heavy silence, the only sound the faint hum of the fluorescent lights overhead. Sarah struggled to find her voice, her throat tight with emotion.

"John," she said softly, "how did you survive?"

He looked at her, his expression hollow. "I don't know. It left me there, broken, bleeding. Maybe it thought I was dead. Maybe it didn't care. But when I woke up, they were gone. All of them."

Nathan stood, his movements deliberate. "That's enough for now," he said, his tone firm but not unkind. "John needs rest."

Sarah wanted to protest, to push for more answers, but she couldn't ignore the exhaustion etched into John's face. She nodded reluctantly, standing as well.

"Thank you," she said quietly, her voice trembling. "For sharing this."

John didn't respond. He turned back to the window, his shoulders slumping as the weight of his grief pressed down on him once more.

Nathan gestured for Sarah to follow him, and together they left the room. As the door closed behind them, Sarah felt the full weight of what she had just heard settle over her. Whatever had taken John's family was still out there—and it wasn't finished.

Shadows in the Cabin

Sarah followed Nathan out of the room, her footsteps heavy against the cold, sterile floor of the nursing home. Her mind buzzed with all that had transpired—the cryptic conversations, John's painful recounting of his family's fate, and the unsettling, unspoken weight hanging in the air. But as they neared the hallway's end, her gaze once again fell on the sleek, metallic cabinet with the glowing keypad.

The temptation to stop and examine it again gnawed at her, but Nathan's looming presence kept her at bay. He was silent, walking beside her, but she could feel his eyes occasionally flicking toward her, as though he knew exactly what she was thinking. As they reached the exit, she paused for a moment, casting one last glance at the cabinet. What's inside there? she wondered, but she knew now wasn't the time.

Outside, the evening air was cold and biting. The sun had set, and the darkness seemed to swallow everything around them. As Sarah made her way to her car, her thoughts churned with the weight of everything she'd learned—and everything she still didn't know. She fumbled with her keys, her hands shaking as she unlocked the door.

Once inside, she let out a deep sigh, trying to calm herself. But the unease wouldn't let her go. She glanced around, her eyes scanning the dimly lit parking lot. Was someone watching her? The sensation of being followed prickled at the back of her neck, a chill crawling down her spine. She started the engine, trying to shake the feeling, but the heaviness lingered.

The drive back to her cabin was quiet, yet her mind was anything but. The winding forest road felt narrower than usual, the trees on either side pressing in as if they too were hiding secrets. Sarah couldn't shake the growing sense of dread that followed her, like an invisible weight pushing down on her chest. Every rustling leaf, every gust of wind felt like a warning.

As she finally pulled into the driveway of her cabin, relief washed over her. But that relief was short-lived. The shadows cast by the tall trees seemed deeper than before, and the isolation of her cabin, once peaceful, now felt like a trap. She hurried inside, locking the door behind her.

With shaky hands, she sat down at her small desk and opened her laptop. Her mind was buzzing, and she needed to distract herself with research. She began searching through online archives, trying to piece together the puzzle of what had happened ten years ago—what had brought John to this place, and what was happening in the reserve now.

The hours slipped by as she scrolled through page after page of articles and obscure reports. Then her phone buzzed on the table, startling her. She grabbed it quickly, seeing the name of her contact flash on the screen. Her heart leapt in her chest.

"Sarah, I dug into the symbol you sent me," the voice on the other end was low, tense. "It's an old military marking. It represents Alpha—the leader, the top of the chain. But that's all I could find. I'm telling you, Sarah, I've already risked too much by looking into this."

"Alpha?" Sarah whispered, her mind racing as she processed the information.

"I can't dig any further. This goes deep, and if I keep poking around, it won't just be my career that's in danger."

Sarah thanked him quietly before hanging up, her mind spinning with the new revelation. She began typing furiously, searching for anything connected to the Alpha symbol. As the pages loaded, she stood up and made her way to the kitchen to brew some coffee.

Just as the water began to boil, a thunderous bang exploded against the front door, shaking the entire cabin. The impact was so strong she felt the pressure in the air, as if something—or someone—had slammed into the door with full force. Her body reacted instinctively, and she threw herself to the floor, heart pounding wildly in her chest. She froze.

Something scratched against the wall outside. The noise was faint, barely there, but enough to send a chill down her spine. Her breath caught in her throat, and she dropped to the floor, trying to stay hidden. Was it her imagination?

A loud, sudden bang echoed through the cabin. The force of it made her heart leap as it rattled the door. The impact felt so strong that she could feel the vibration in the air around her. Sarah pressed herself flat against the floor, her hands trembling as her mind raced.

The sound of footsteps followed, circling the perimeter of the cabin, each one slow, deliberate, almost taunting. Her pulse quickened. She held her breath, her body frozen in fear, as the scraping noise returned, this time closer—just outside the window.

Then, just as suddenly as it had started, the noise stopped.

Sarah remained on the floor, too terrified to move. Minutes passed, stretching into what felt like hours before she finally dared to stand up. She crept to the window, peeking out into the dark. Nothing. The forest was still, eerily silent.

But something was wrong. She hurried back to her desk, her hands trembling as she reached for her coffee cup—only to see her computer screen flickering. A message had appeared, anonymous, ominous:

"If anything happens, call this number."

Her heart thudded in her chest. How had someone sent this message? Who was it? She felt a surge of fear wash over her as she glanced around the room, suddenly feeling exposed and vulnerable. Her fingers were shaking. Whoever this is, they're watching me…

She hurried to check the locks on the doors and windows, ensuring everything was sealed tight before plunging the cabin into complete darkness. She retreated to her bed, clutching her phone and laptop as she curled up in the corner, the weight of fear pressing down on her. Every creak, every gust of wind outside made her flinch.

She typed back a message to the anonymous contact: "Who are you? What's going on?"

The reply came almost immediately, as though someone was sitting right beside her: "Be careful. This isn't something to mess with."

Sarah's pulse quickened. She hesitated before typing again: "Nathan?"

The screen remained silent, but then the number from the earlier message flashed again. Sarah programmed it into her phone with trembling hands. Whoever this is, they know more than I do…

Exhaustion weighed on her, but her mind refused to calm down. Sleep came only in short, fitful bursts, and every sound outside jolted her awake. When she finally opened her eyes the next morning, sunlight filtered through the curtains, casting long shadows across the floor.

But something was wrong.

Whispers of Alpha

As she peered through the window, her breath caught. The same car she had seen at the nursing home was now parked beside hers, standing eerily alone in the quiet of the woods.

Sarah quickly dressed and threw on her jacket, stepping outside into the crisp morning air. She scanned the area, her heart thudding in her chest. There was no sign of Nathan, but she knew he was nearby. Why is he here?

She called out his name, her voice echoing through the trees. No response. But as she turned to head back inside, Nathan appeared, emerging from the treeline. His face was unreadable as he walked toward her.

Without a word, he gestured for her to follow, leading her to the back of the cabin. There, scratched deep into the wooden walls, were massive claw marks—long, jagged slashes that tore through the timber.

Nathan turned to her, his expression grave. "You've got two choices," he said coldly. "You can pack up and leave right now, or you can come with me to John."

Sarah stared at him, her pulse racing. "What the hell is going on here, Nathan?" she demanded, her voice shaking with frustration and fear.

Nathan's gaze was sharp, filled with a seriousness that chilled her to the bone. "Something you don't want to be dealing with," he replied, his tone dark. “Something out of your worst nightmares.”

Without another word, Sarah ran inside, frantically packing up her most important belongings. Her hands trembled as she threw her things into a bag, and when she finally zipped it shut, she bolted for the door.

Her mind raced, questions flooding her thoughts, but one thing was certain: she had to get out of here. Fast. Nathan drove ahead, his car navigating the winding road with ease as Sarah followed close behind. The early morning light filtered through the trees, casting long shadows that danced across the path. The forest was quiet, save for the occasional rustle of leaves in the breeze. But the silence didn’t soothe her—if anything, it made everything feel more tense. The winding road, the trees closing in, the weight of what was coming—it all pressed down on her like a heavy fog.

What am I doing?

The thought echoed louder now, more urgent. She wasn’t just investigating anymore; she was in the middle of something dark and dangerous, and she didn’t even know how deep it went. Her hands tightened on the steering wheel as she tried to focus on the road, but her mind kept spinning.

John’s hollow eyes, Nathan’s cryptic warnings, the mysterious Alpha—everything pointed to something much bigger than she had anticipated. Alpha. That word lingered in her thoughts, tugging at her.

What is Alpha? Why does it matter so much?

The road curved ahead, and Sarah's foot eased off the gas pedal. The light filtering through the trees grew harsher, casting sharp contrasts across the path. She spotted a small turnout—a rest area off the road—and without thinking, she veered toward it, pulling the car over. As the engine quieted, she sat there for a moment, gripping the steering wheel and trying to calm the frantic thoughts racing through her mind.

She stepped out of the car, the crisp morning air hitting her skin, grounding her for a moment. Leaning against the hood, she tried to take deep breaths, but her thoughts wouldn't settle. Is it after me now, too? The thing that had destroyed John's family, the thing hunting in the shadows—was it now coming for her?

Her mind flashed back to the night outside her cabin. The scratching, the footsteps, the overwhelming feeling of being watched. Whatever it was, it hadn't been human, and the thought sent a chill down her spine.

Behind her, the sound of another car pulling over made her turn. Nathan had stopped his vehicle as well, and he was walking toward her with calm, measured steps.

"Everything okay?" he asked, his voice steady but laced with an unspoken understanding.

Sarah looked up at him, her chest tight with frustration. "Alpha," she said, the word bursting out. "Is that what this is about? Alpha?" Her voice wavered with a mix of anger and confusion.

Nathan watched her for a moment, his face unreadable. Then he sighed, glancing away toward the trees. "Alpha is nothing you want to be involved with," he said, his voice quieter but firm. "There's a reason people are afraid to even say the name. It's not something you can understand without seeing it."

Sarah felt her pulse quicken. "Then why don't you tell me? You know more than you're letting on."

Nathan's gaze shifted back to her, sharp and calculating. "Because once you understand, there's no going back. And if anyone can make you understand, it's John. He's the only one who survived."

The weight of his words pressed down on her, and for a moment, she felt a heavy knot form in her stomach. John… the only survivor. It sounded like the plot of some nightmare, but she was living it now.

"You still have two choices," Nathan said, his voice cutting through her thoughts. "You can turn around and drive away from all of this, or you can follow me and hear what John has to say. But once you choose, there's no turning back."

Sarah stared at him, her thoughts racing. She could turn around right now, leave all of this behind, but how could she? How could she walk away from this story, from the truth that had eluded so many?

Without a word, she pushed off the hood of her car and slid back into the driver's seat. For a moment, she rested her head against the steering wheel, muttering to herself, "This is a nightmare."

The forest around her was peaceful, almost too peaceful, the kind of peace that felt like a warning. How has something like this stayed hidden for so long? The world had moved on, ignoring whatever terror lurked beneath the surface. And now, she was caught in the middle of it.

She thought back to her visit to the archives. People walking through the streets, unaware of what she was about to uncover. But as soon as she had stepped into the archive, the air had shifted—something dark and unseen had followed her. The eerie receptionist, the empty streets when she had left, her contact's sudden fear… and now this. Even someone who wasn't afraid to leak government secrets was terrified to speak of Alpha.

Sarah clenched her hands around the wheel. What could be so dangerous that it silenced even the bravest of sources? And what had she gotten herself into by digging this deep?

Nathan stood by his car, watching her with his usual guarded expression. She wasn't sure if he was waiting for her to change her mind, but she knew her decision had already been made.

With a deep breath, Sarah started the engine and followed Nathan back onto the road. The trees pressed in on both sides as they drove deeper into the woods, the morning light filtering through the branches, casting ghostly patterns on the road.

Beyond the Fence

The high chain-link fence came into view, its barbed wire glinting faintly in the pale morning light. Sarah gripped the steering wheel tighter as the car approached, a knot of unease twisting in her stomach. She had seen the fence before, but its imposing height and the countless cameras mounted along its perimeter still unnerved her. What kind of nursing home needed this level of security?

Nathan slowed his car just ahead, pulling to a stop before the gates. Sarah's car idled behind his, and she watched him through her windshield. His movements were precise as he retrieved his phone, speaking in low tones that didn't carry back to her. From her seat, the fence seemed to stretch endlessly, vanishing into the dense trees that shrouded the area. It was more than a barrier—it was a statement.

Is this place meant to keep someone inside, or something out? The thought gnawed at her, a shadow over her already restless mind.

With a groan of metal and a faint screech, the gates slowly slid open. Nathan's car moved forward, and Sarah reluctantly followed. The resounding thud of the gates locking behind her made her flinch. She couldn't shake the feeling that she'd just crossed a threshold she couldn't return from.

The parking lot ahead was small, bordered by the tree line on one side and the sleek, clinical building on the other. As Sarah parked next to Nathan's car, she scanned the area. The unnatural quiet was suffocating. No wind stirred the trees, no birdsong broke the silence. It was as if the world outside this place didn't exist.

Sarah's thoughts slipped back to her cabin—the deafening bang on the door, the scraping sounds outside, and Nathan's sudden appearance. Her chest tightened. She had come here seeking answers, but now she wasn't sure she wanted to know them.

A knock on her window startled her. Nathan stood outside, his expression calm but firm. "John's waiting," he said, his tone carrying an edge of urgency.

Sarah took a deep breath, steeling herself. Exhaustion weighed her down, but the knot of curiosity and determination kept her moving. She opened the door, stepping into the crisp morning air. It bit at her skin, sharp and grounding.

Nathan walked to the back of his car, opening the trunk with a practiced ease. He pulled out a black backpack, the motion smooth and deliberate. Sarah's unease deepened. Everything about him—his posture, his actions, his tone—felt too controlled, too calculated. This wasn't just a visit; it was an operation.

As Nathan turned to her, he spoke with calm authority. "You coming?"

Sarah bit her lip, her frustration bubbling to the surface. "It's strange, isn't it?" she said, her voice shaky but pointed. "I know nothing about you, but you seem to know everything about me. You show up at my cabin after the worst night of my life, and now this…" She gestured toward the nursing home. "Why can't you just tell me what's going on?"

For a moment, Nathan's gaze softened, but the barrier between them remained. Without answering, he turned and walked toward the entrance, leaving Sarah standing by her car. Her frustration boiled over.

"Why?!" she called after him, her voice sharp and raw. But Nathan didn't stop. His measured steps infuriated her, the indifference in his demeanor pushing her closer to the edge.

As he reached the doors, Nathan glanced back over his shoulder. "Don't forget your bag," he said, his tone maddeningly casual.

Sarah slammed her car door harder than she intended, grabbing her bag from the passenger seat. Her fists clenched around the straps as she hurried to catch up. The stillness of the place pressed down on her, each step toward the building feeling heavier than the last.

At the entrance, Sarah blocked Nathan's path, her frustration spilling over. "Why are you doing this?" she demanded, her voice trembling. "Why can't you just tell me the truth? What the hell am I walking into?"

Nathan stopped, meeting her gaze with a calm that bordered on unsettling. For a fleeting second, something flickered in his expression —a hesitation, a crack in his armor. "Sarah," he said quietly, "some things are better left unsaid. What's inside… John is the only one who can help you understand."

His words landed heavily, their weight sinking into her chest. Sarah's resolve faltered, but she forced herself to take a steadying breath.

Whatever this was, she had come too far to turn back now.

With a weary sigh, she followed Nathan through the double doors. Each step felt like a descent into an abyss, the air thick with unspoken secrets. The building's interior was as clinical as its exterior—sterile walls painted a drab green, fluorescent lights flickering faintly overhead. The smell of antiseptic mixed with a faint metallic tang that sent a chill down Sarah's spine.

Nathan's footsteps echoed sharply against the linoleum floor, steady and unhurried. Sarah's heavier steps followed, her emotions betraying her. She struggled to match his composed pace, her mind racing with questions she wasn't sure she wanted answers to.

A sudden buzz from Nathan's phone broke the oppressive silence. He slowed his stride, pulling the device from his pocket without breaking his calm demeanor.

"Ward," he answered, his tone clipped. The faint echo of his voice carried down the corridor, the words too low for Sarah to make out.

She slowed her pace, straining to catch any detail of the conversation. Nathan's expression remained unreadable, his responses brief and measured.

"Understood," he said after a pause. "Maintain the perimeter and keep comms open. I'll handle it."

As he ended the call and slipped the phone back into his pocket, Sarah couldn't hold back any longer. "Who was that?" she demanded, her voice sharp. “And don’t tell me it’s none of my business.”

Nathan turned to face her, his calm exterior unbroken. “They wanted to make sure arrangements were in place,” he said simply.

Sarah scoffed, her frustration boiling over. “Arrangements? For what? My funeral?”

Nathan’s eyes narrowed slightly, the faintest hint of irritation crossing his features. “No,” he said, stepping closer. “For your hotel room tonight.”

Sarah blinked, momentarily thrown off. “Hotel room? Who are ‘they’?!”

Nathan tilted his head, his expression almost amused. But beneath the surface, there was something darker. “People who want you to stay alive.”

His words hit her like a punch to the gut. Her voice rose, cutting through the sterile corridor. “Oh, fantastic. Mysterious people who think they know what’s best for me. Great. Just great. Who the hell are these people, Nathan? And why are they treating me like a pawn?”

Nathan’s voice dropped to a near whisper, though its intensity sent a chill through her. “Enough,” he said firmly. “You want answers? Fine. But don’t mistake their concern—or mine—for control. If you want to walk into this blind, be my guest.”

Before Sarah could respond, the creak of a door opening drew their attention. John stepped into the corridor, his face pale and weary. He leaned against the doorframe, his eyes darting between Sarah and Nathan.

"Is… everything okay here?" John asked hesitantly, his voice tinged with concern.

Nathan's demeanor shifted, his usual sharpness softening slightly. "Just a misunderstanding," he said, his tone even. "Sarah needed some clarification."

Sarah crossed her arms, glaring at Nathan. "Clarification? Yeah, like who these mysterious 'they' people are that apparently have my best interests at heart."

John's expression darkened slightly as he looked at Sarah. "Trust is hard to come by," he said softly. "But Nathan's not the enemy."

Sarah let out a bitter laugh, throwing up her hands. "Oh, sure. The guy who refuses to give me a straight answer isn't the enemy. He's just the gatekeeper to all the things I'm not allowed to know."

Nathan's voice cut through her frustration like a blade. "You're not ready to know everything. Not yet."

John's gaze softened, his hand resting lightly on Sarah's shoulder. "Whatever this is," he said gently, "we need to focus on what's ahead. Sarah, you'll need every ounce of clarity you can get."

Nathan turned, his composure unshaken. "The room's already paid for," he said over his shoulder. "Stay or don't. But if you're smart, you'll take the out they're offering."

Sarah stared after him, her fists clenched at her sides. The fluorescent lights above flickered, casting harsh shadows against the walls. Somewhere deeper in the building, the faint beep of a heart monitor echoed, a haunting reminder of the fragility of life.

John's voice broke the silence, calm and measured. "I've made some coffee. Let's talk inside."

For the first time, Sarah felt a sliver of solace in his tone. She nodded, her anger receding into exhaustion, and followed him into his room. Whatever waited beyond the next door, she knew it was only the beginning of the answers she sought

Beneath the Surface

The room John led her to was a stark contrast to the hallway. A soft, warm light from a desk lamp filled the space, its amber glow reflecting off the beige walls. The faint aroma of freshly brewed coffee hung in the air, a small reprieve from the sterile smells outside.

Nathan was already seated in a worn chair by the corner, his posture relaxed but his eyes sharp. He held a steaming mug, the rising vapors blurring his angular features. His gaze followed them as they entered, assessing but unreadable.

John set Sarah's bag down gently by the door and handed her a mug of coffee. She accepted it with a quiet nod, the warmth of the ceramic sinking into her chilled fingers.

"Take a seat, Sarah," John said gently. "You'll feel better with some coffee."

Sarah hesitated for a moment before lowering herself into a chair near the table. The upholstery let out a soft creak as she settled in. The room was quiet, save for the faint hum of the muted TV in the background. She stared down into the coffee, its dark surface reflecting her own tired face.

"I always wanted to be a reporter," Sarah began, her voice quiet, almost as if she didn't want the room to hear her. "It's all I ever dreamed of."

John leaned forward slightly, his forearms resting on his knees, his hands clasped. His silence felt inviting, a nudge for her to continue.

"When I got this assignment… I thought it was my big chance. Something real. Something that mattered." She exhaled shakily, placing the mug down on the table as her hands began to tremble. "But it's all a joke, isn't it? None of it makes sense. I'm just… chasing shadows."

Nathan tilted his head slightly, his gaze still fixed on her. "Everyone starts somewhere, Sarah. This just… happens to be a bigger somewhere than most."

His words carried a calm reassurance, but his tone remained pragmatic. Sarah let out a hollow laugh, shaking her head. "Bigger? It's chaos. Nothing in journalism school prepared me for… this."

John cleared his throat, his voice steady but heavy. "Sometimes, chaos is the only way to find the truth. And sometimes…" His voice faltered slightly. "…the truth doesn't come without a cost."

The muted TV continued its steady hum in the background, its images cycling through bleak news stories. Sarah stared at the screen, her fingers tightening around the remote.

"This is what I wanted. To be in the middle of the story. But why does it feel like I'm drowning in it?"

Nathan didn't respond immediately, his gaze fixed on the screen. "Because you're asking the right questions. And sometimes, the right questions don't have easy answers."

Sarah exhaled sharply and pressed the remote, switching the channel. The screen changed to a history program, the rich tones of a narrator filling the room.

"...and so the Beast of Gévaudan terrorized the French countryside in the 1700s. A creature of myth and legend that defied explanation..."

The screen displayed a grainy image of an old painting—a monstrous creature with glowing eyes, twisted limbs, and razor-sharp teeth. Sarah didn't flinch, but across the table, John froze. His breath caught in his throat, and the color drained from his face.

The mug in his hand trembled violently, its edge tapping against the table with a faint clink. His eyes widened, fixed on the screen as if the creature might leap out at any moment.

Nathan noticed instantly. In one swift motion, he rose from his chair and crossed the room, switching off the TV with a deliberate press of the button. The room fell into heavy silence.

"What the hell, Nathan?!" Sarah started, startled.

Nathan didn't answer. His attention remained on John, whose breathing was shallow and labored.

"I was there..." John whispered, his voice barely audible.

Sarah stared at him, her voice rising in confusion. "Where? What are you talking about? Where were you?"

John's trembling hands gripped the edge of the table, his voice breaking as he spoke. "I was there when my wife... my youngest son... and my daughter were taken from me. I couldn't do anything."

The air in the room seemed to freeze, heavy with the weight of his words. Sarah sat back, stunned into silence, while Nathan moved closer to John.

"John, take it from the beginning," Nathan said calmly, his tone low but commanding. "Everything in its time."

John exhaled shakily, his voice dropping to a whisper. "A rescue team found me. They pulled me out when I had nothing left. But they couldn't..." He paused, his voice breaking. "...they couldn't save them."

Nathan placed a steadying hand on John's shoulder. "You don't have to carry this alone, John. Not anymore."

The room remained silent, the hum of the distant hallway the only sound as Sarah processed what she had just heard. John leaned forward, his hands clasped so tightly his knuckles turned white. His face bore the weight of untold grief, his voice emerging low and cracked, like the sound of splintering wood under pressure.

"I wanted to surprise them... my wife, my kids. They deserved something good, something pure. I thought... maybe if I took them somewhere untouched by the world's chaos, we could... we could start fresh."

His voice broke, and for a moment, he seemed lost in a memory too sharp to escape. The room held its breath as Sarah's gentle tone broke the silence.

"But something felt off, didn't it?" she asked softly.

John's nod was almost imperceptible, his throat working as if forcing down a tide of emotions.

"We got there late in the afternoon. The light was soft, golden, the kind that makes the world look… safe. There was a line at the gates. I didn't think much of it—people looking to get away like us. But then we heard… the ranger was missing. They wouldn't say how or why, just… gone. They called in a reserve officer to take over."

He lapsed into silence, his hands gripping the edges of his knees like a lifeline. The air grew heavier, thick with the weight of what wasn't being said.

"The next morning, I found tracks circling our camp," John continued, his voice faltering. "Huge ones. Like a wolf, but wrong. Too large, too deep. And the claws… they looked like fingers."

He fell silent, the room heavy with tension. Nathan, who had been quietly observing, finally spoke. "Sarah, your ride is here. Let's give John some space."

Sarah snapped, "Now? In the middle of this? I need answers, Nathan."

Nathan's eyes met hers, steady. "And you'll get them. But not all at once. Let's go."

Reluctantly, Sarah stood, glancing back at John. "Thank you for sharing this. I know it wasn't easy."

John gave her a faint nod, his shoulders slumping under the weight of his memories. Nathan picked up her bag at the door and gestured for her to follow.

As they exited into the early afternoon, the sunlight pierced through the dense trees, casting long, shifting shadows across the parking lot. The warmth of the day felt misplaced, a contrast to the tension that lingered between them. The gravel crunched underfoot, breaking the oppressive silence as they neared the far end of the lot.

Parked there was a sleek black SUV, its paint glinting faintly in the sunlight. Flanking the vehicle were two figures dressed in dark suits. They stood like sentinels, their expressions unreadable, their postures deceptively relaxed. Sarah's sharp eyes didn't miss the faint bulge under their jackets—holstered weapons, ready for use.

Her steps slowed, unease prickling at the back of her neck. Nathan stopped just before the car, turning briefly toward her. Without waiting for her to speak, he opened the back door, his demeanor as composed as ever.

Sarah hesitated, her hand clutching the strap of her bag. "This… hotel they've booked for me. Who are 'they,' exactly?" she asked, her voice steady but edged with suspicion.

Nathan's lips twitched slightly, not quite forming a smile. "People who want to make sure you're safe."

"Safe from what?" she pressed, narrowing her eyes.

For a moment, he didn't answer. His gaze flicked past her, scanning the tree line. Then, his voice came low and measured, almost amused. "Safe from the unknown."

Before she could push further, the faint buzz of a phone cut through the stillness. Nathan pulled the device from his pocket, his expression shifting imperceptibly as he read the caller ID.

"Job call?" Sarah asked, her curiosity edging into irritation.

He didn't reply. Instead, he stepped back, placing his hand firmly on the car door. His sharp eyes met hers for a brief second before he swung the door shut with a decisive click. Turning away, he lifted the phone to his ear as he walked back toward the building, his voice low and inaudible.

From inside the SUV, Sarah watched him disappear into the shadows of the nursing home. The two suited men exchanged a glance but said nothing, their attention shifting back to the perimeter. The silence pressed against her, and as the engine hummed to life, she couldn't shake the sense that the answers she sought were slipping further from her grasp.

Truth

Inside the hospital, Nathan made his way to the roof, his phone pressed to his ear.

"What's the situation?" Nathan's voice was calm but laced with an edge of urgency.

A static-laden reply came through, the tension palpable even through the interference.

"Movement detected near the last known coordinates. Satellite is tracking now."

Nathan's jaw tightened as he reached the rooftop. The faint sound of rotor blades grew louder, the rhythmic thrum cutting through the still air. Moments later, a helicopter descended, its downdraft whipping through his hair and ruffling his coat. Nathan stepped forward as the craft landed, his expression unreadable.

From behind, a familiar voice broke through the din. "Job?"

Nathan turned to see John standing there, his hands buried deep in his coat pockets, a shadow of concern crossing his face.

"Yeah," Nathan replied simply, his gaze softening slightly.

John hesitated, his shoulders tensing. "Be careful out there. You're... you're important to us."

Nathan's lips pressed into a thin line, and he gave a curt nod. "I'll be back."

With that, he climbed into the helicopter. The engine roared to life, the wind picking up as the craft lifted off. John remained on the rooftop, watching as the helicopter disappeared into the horizon, his face etched with quiet worry.

Meanwhile, Sarah sat in the back of the SUV, her mind racing as the city blurred past the tinted windows. The agents in the front seat had been silent, their terse responses offering little in the way of comfort or explanation. The tension gnawed at her, frustration bubbling under the surface.

"You know," she began, her tone laced with irritation, "it's been pretty quiet in here. Is this how things always are?"

One of the agents barely glanced back at her, his voice flat. "We stick to protocol."

Sarah sighed heavily, leaning back against the leather seat. Protocol. That word again. It was as if every part of this situation had been meticulously planned, leaving her with nothing but questions and no one willing to answer them.

Her thoughts drifted back to John's warnings—the massive footprints, the unnatural silence in the forest. Was it all connected? And where did Nathan fit into this tangled web of secrets? His guarded demeanor, his cryptic comments—what was he hiding?

As the car cruised down the empty highway, unease settled over her like a heavy blanket. She glanced at the two agents in the front seat. Their stoic silence was unnerving, as if they'd been trained to ignore her.

"Perfect," she muttered under her breath, "they won't even look me in the eye. Just like Nathan. What kind of game is this?"

Her mind lingered on the image of the footprints John had described. She could almost see them—deep, claw-like impressions in the dirt, too massive to belong to any known animal. The thought sent a shiver down her spine. Had something been watching him that night? And did Nathan know more than he was letting on?

The SUV slowed as they entered a quieter part of the city. The buildings here were sleek and modern, but the emptiness of the streets added to the eerie atmosphere. As they pulled into the hotel driveway, Sarah's chest tightened. Everything felt too controlled, too deliberate.

Two heavily armed guards stood at the entrance, their sharp eyes scanning the surroundings. One of them opened the car door for her, his movements efficient and impersonal. Sarah stepped out, her unease growing as she took in her surroundings.

The hotel was pristine, its polished glass facade reflecting the late afternoon sun. Inside, the air was cool and sterile, the lobby exuding an unsettling perfection. Another agent approached her, his demeanor as impassive as the others.

“Do I even need to check in, or is everything already taken care of?” Sarah asked, sarcasm dripping from her tone.

“Everything has been arranged,” the agent replied, his voice devoid of emotion.

Sarah clenched her jaw, resisting the urge to lash out. The constant feeling of being managed, controlled, was suffocating. She followed the agent through the lobby, every step amplifying her frustration. The walls seemed to close in around her, each polished surface reflecting her growing sense of entrapment.

As they stepped into an elevator, the doors slid shut with a soft hiss, enclosing them in tense silence. The elevator ascended smoothly, stopping at the top floor. When the doors opened, an immaculately dressed hotel employee greeted them, leading Sarah down a long, carpeted hallway.

“Why all this secrecy? All this security?” Sarah asked aloud, her voice sharp with frustration. “I’m not some target.”

The employee glanced at her briefly before replying, “It’s Nathan’s request. Maximum security. His decision.”

Sarah stopped in her tracks, staring at the door ahead of her. Nathan. His name felt like a key to a puzzle she couldn’t solve. Everything about this situation was orchestrated, designed to keep her in the dark.

“What does Nathan have to hide?” she muttered as she entered the room.

The suite was immaculate, the kind of luxurious space that felt more like a prison than a refuge. Sarah dropped her bag by the bed and moved to the desk, her frustration bubbling over. She opened her laptop, her fingers flying across the keyboard as she searched for answers. Typing "Nathan Wards" yielded nothing. No records, no history. It was as if he didn't exist.

"Why is there nothing on him?" she whispered, her voice tinged with disbelief. "Where are all the answers?"

Desperate, she called her contact, asking him to dig into Nathan's background. Minutes later, the response came, low and urgent.

"There are many with that name," her contact said. "But… there's something strange. I found a profile. It's him, isn't it?"

Sarah nodded, her fingers trembling as she opened the file her contact sent. The photo was unmistakable. Nathan, but much younger. Her stomach churned as she read the accompanying details.

"Is this… really him?" she asked, her voice shaking.

Her contact's voice grew quieter, more urgent. "If this is Nathan Wards, he's been dead for over ten years. He disappeared during a mission. His family assumed he was killed in action. He was a legend—a top-tier medic, saved countless lives. But he vanished without a trace."

Sarah sat back in her chair, the weight of the revelation pressing down on her. It wasn't just that Nathan had a past—it was the fact that his past shouldn't even exist.

"What happened to you, Nathan?" she whispered, her mind racing with questions she wasn't sure she wanted answered.

Breaking the Barrier

The old SUV rattled to a stop just short of the forest's edge, its headlights casting eerie beams that barely penetrated the dense wall of trees marking the boundary of the reserve. Inside, the group of five friends—Connor, Ellie, Megan, Ryan, and Jake—laughed and joked, their chatter masking the uneasy quiet outside. The air was thick with anticipation, the kind that comes from doing something they all knew was a bad idea.

Connor, seated in the driver's seat, turned toward the others with his trademark confident smirk. As the oldest and the self-proclaimed leader, he thrived on pushing boundaries. He clapped his hands sharply, drawing their attention.

"Alright, listen up," he announced. "This is going to be a night to remember. All those stories about weird shit happening here? Government propaganda, plain and simple. They just don't want people poking around."

Ellie, seated in the back, shifted uncomfortably. Her voice was soft but firm. "What if it's not just stories, Connor? What if there really is something going on out here?"

Connor laughed, turning to face her fully. "Ellie, you've got to stop watching horror movies. I've been coming here since I was a kid. Do you know how many monsters I've seen? Zero. Nada. It's all in people's heads."

Megan, sitting beside Ellie, let out an exaggerated sigh and rolled her eyes. "Ellie, relax. Nothing's going to happen. This is just Connor being Connor. You know how he is."

Ryan, in the passenger seat, glanced back with a small, reassuring smile. "If it gets too creepy, we'll head back, alright? Don't let him get to you."

Ellie nodded reluctantly, though her arms stayed crossed tightly over her chest. She didn't want to ruin the mood, but something about the forest made her skin crawl.

Meanwhile, Jake, the youngest of the group and seated on the far side of Ellie, rummaged through the cooler at his feet. He cracked open a beer with a wry grin. "We've got snacks, drinks, and a terrible idea. What could possibly go wrong?"

Connor snorted and threw open his door. "Nothing, because we're not about to let a little imagination stop us." He shot a pointed look at Ellie before stepping out of the car.

The others followed, grabbing their gear from the trunk: backpacks filled with snacks, bottles of liquor, a Bluetooth speaker, and blankets. Connor slung a bolt cutter over his shoulder, holding it up triumphantly.

"Ladies and gentlemen," he said with a mock bow. "Your VIP access to adventure awaits."

As the group trudged toward the fence, the atmosphere shifted. The air grew colder, and a heavy silence seemed to press down on them. The forest loomed ahead like a solid wall of shadows, its presence both imposing and unnerving. Every rustle of leaves or snap of a twig made Ellie flinch.

"Did it have to be this place?" she muttered under her breath.

"Hell yeah," Connor replied as they reached the chain-link fence. "The farther we are from civilization, the better. That's what makes it fun."

Ellie's stomach churned as Connor crouched to cut through the fence. The sharp snap of metal echoed unnaturally loud in the stillness, making her wince.

"I don't know, Connor," Megan said, her bravado faltering. "Are you sure this is a good idea? What if someone catches us?"

Connor rolled his eyes, his tone dripping with exasperation. "Megan, the entire reserve is supposed to be evacuated. There's no one here but us. Now stop worrying and get through the damn fence."

He held the flap open, his grin challenging them to back down.

Ellie hesitated, staring into the black maw of the forest. Her instincts screamed at her to turn around, to get back in the car and leave. But the weight of her friends' stares pushed her forward.

"Fine," she muttered, ducking through the gap.

One by one, the others followed, their flashlights slicing through the oppressive darkness. Connor brought up the rear, tossing the bolt cutter into his bag with a satisfied grin.

As they ventured deeper into the woods, the shadows seemed to close in around them, and even Connor's easy confidence began to waver. But none of them said a word about the sudden chill in the air or the way the trees seemed to watch their every move. They couldn't shake the feeling that something—or someone—was waiting for them, just beyond the reach of their lights.

Shadows in the Fire - Part 1

The trail they followed was faint, overgrown with moss and leaves. Their voices seemed unnaturally loud in the eerie quiet, a stark contrast to the oppressive stillness of the forest. Ellie couldn't shake the feeling that they were being watched. Each time she turned her flashlight behind them, nothing was there.

"Ellie, you look like you've seen a ghost," Jake teased, nudging her. "Relax. It's just trees and squirrels."

"Yeah, Ellie," Connor added with a smirk. "Or maybe Bigfoot. Either way, we're safe."

"You don't know that," she shot back, her tone sharper than intended.

Connor raised his hands in mock surrender. "Alright, alright. But seriously, stop freaking yourself out. You're going to ruin the vibe."

They trudged on, their footsteps crunching against gravel and fallen leaves. Finally, they emerged into a clearing where a small fire pit surrounded by stones sat waiting for them. Nearby, an abandoned ranger's jeep loomed, its windows streaked with dirt.

"See?" Connor said, spreading his arms. "Perfect spot. And look—free firewood."

He yanked the jeep's trunk open, pulling out a bundle of dried logs.

“Is this… okay?” Megan asked, her voice barely audible. “I mean, what if this is someone’s stuff?”

Connor shot her a look. “It’s not. If they cared, they’d be here, wouldn’t they?”

Ryan shook his head but said nothing, helping Connor arrange the logs in the pit. Within minutes, flames roared to life, casting flickering light across their faces.

Ellie sat on the edge of the group, her arms wrapped tightly around her knees. The warmth of the fire did little to soothe her nerves, and she couldn’t shake the feeling that the darkness beyond the clearing was alive.

“Ellie,” Ryan called, offering her a beer.

She shook her head. “I’m fine.”

“Suit yourself,” Connor said, cracking open another drink. “But don’t start with the ghost stories. We’re here to have fun, not play Scooby-Doo.”

The conversation drifted as the night wore on. They laughed, told stories, and passed around drinks, but Ellie’s unease only grew. She watched as shadows shifted at the edge of the firelight, as if the forest itself was breathing.

The first snap of a branch made her jump.

“What was that?” she whispered.

Connor waved her off. “Relax. Probably a deer.”

But Ellie wasn’t convinced. Her eyes darted around the clearing, scanning the darkness for movement.

“It’s nothing,” Jake stretched his arms, a lazy grin plastered across his face as he stood near the fire. The flames flickered, painting eerie shadows on the surrounding trees.

“Man, I need to take a leak,” he announced, his voice nonchalant as he grabbed his flashlight.

Ellie’s head snapped up from where she sat. “Are you sure that's a good idea? It’s so dark out there, Jake.”

Connor laughed, shaking his head. “Ellie, he’s not wandering into Mordor. He’s taking a piss, not joining a search party.”

Megan smirked, nudging Ellie. “You worry too much. Go ahead, Jake, just don’t get lost out there.”

“Don’t worry, Mom,” Jake said with a mock salute, his flashlight slicing through the darkness. He stumbled slightly as he walked, the remnants of his earlier beers evident.

“If you hear a bear growling, just run faster than Connor,” Ryan called after him, earning a chorus of laughter from the group—except Ellie, whose hands tightened around her knees.

Jake disappeared into the treeline, his steps crunching against the forest floor until the sound faded. Ellie's gaze followed him, unease prickling at the back of her neck.

"Why do you always have to make jokes about this stuff?" she muttered, glancing at Connor.

"Because it's harmless," he replied with a shrug. "You're seriously acting like something's gonna jump out and grab him. Chill, Ellie."

Jake stumbled over a root, catching himself with one hand against the bark of a tree. He chuckled to himself, muttering under his breath. "These trees need to watch where they're going," he joked, shining his flashlight around. The pale beam revealed the undergrowth, nothing more than tangled weeds and scattered leaves.

He found a slight incline and trudged up, stopping near a sturdy tree. The forest around him felt unnervingly still, the usual hum of nocturnal life conspicuously absent.

"Guess even the crickets have bedtime," he muttered, unzipping his pants and relieving himself.

For a moment, the silence wrapped around him like a heavy blanket. Then he felt it—a faint vibration in his chest, almost imperceptible at first.

Jake froze, his brow furrowing. The vibration grew, resonating through his ribcage like the low purr of an engine. He glanced around, his flashlight beam darting across the forest, finding nothing but shadows.

"Nice try, guys!" he shouted, his voice cracking slightly. "Real original. What are you, hiding behind a tree? Come on out!"

No response.

The vibration intensified, accompanied by a deep, guttural sound—like the growl of something impossibly large.

Jake's breath hitched. He zipped up his pants hastily, his hands trembling. "Alright, enough with the games! This isn't funny!"

He spun around, shining his flashlight in every direction. The beam landed on nothing but darkness. Then, just at the edge of the light's reach, he saw it.

Two glowing red orbs, hovering in the blackness.

Jake's heart plummeted, his pulse pounding in his ears. The eyes were fixed on him, unblinking and impossibly vivid. He couldn't move. His body felt locked in place, as though an invisible force had wrapped around him.

"What the…" he whispered, his voice barely audible.

The vibration in his chest became a tangible pressure, each low rumble like a physical blow. Jake tried to swallow, but his throat felt dry, his legs frozen beneath him.

Then the thing stepped closer.

The eyes came into sharper focus, and behind them, jagged teeth glinted in the faint light. A chilling grin stretched across its face, each razor-sharp fang glistening with malice.

Jake wanted to scream, but his voice caught in his throat. His muscles refused to respond. It was as though the thing's very presence had stripped him of all control.

The grin widened.

Jake finally managed a scream—a raw, primal sound that tore through the stillness of the night.

Shadows in the Fire - Part 2

Everyone around the fire froze, their heads snapping toward the direction of the scream. Ellie shot to her feet, clutching her jacket tightly around her. "Did you hear that?" she asked, her voice trembling.

Connor, leaning lazily against a fallen log, snorted. "It's just Jake being Jake. Probably stepped on a twig and freaked himself out."

Ellie's wide eyes darted between the treeline and Connor. "That didn't sound like a joke, Connor. It sounded… wrong."

Megan exchanged a glance with Ryan, shrugging. "Jake loves to mess with people. It's probably his way of keeping us on edge. Classic Jake."

Ryan chuckled, draining his beer. "Yeah, dude's probably crouched behind a tree waiting for us to come looking." He nudged Megan. "C'mon, let's give him a taste of his own medicine."

Megan hesitated, brushing dirt off her jeans. "You sure? Ellie looks pretty freaked out."

Connor waved dismissively, a smirk playing on his lips. "Jake's fine. Ellie just spooks easy. Don't let her ruin the fun."

Ellie turned to him, frustration flashing in her eyes. "This isn't about fun, Connor. What if he's hurt? What if—"

Connor cut her off with an exaggerated groan. "He's not hurt, Ellie.

Relax. Let them handle it." He gestured toward Ryan and Megan, who were already preparing to head into the woods.

Ryan grabbed a flashlight from his pack, grinning. "Don't worry, Ellie. If Jake's just screwing around, I'll scare him so bad he won't try it again. Right, Megan?"

Megan smirked but cast a wary glance toward Ellie. "We'll be back in a minute. Keep the fire going."

Ellie looked to Connor for support, her voice quieter now. "We shouldn't split up. This… this doesn't feel right."

Connor stretched his legs out, his tone dismissive. "You're overthinking it. Jake's probably doubled over laughing right now, thinking he's scared us all. Let Ryan and Megan deal with it."

Sighing, Ellie wrapped her arms tightly around herself as Ryan and Megan disappeared into the dense trees. Their laughter faded quickly, swallowed by the oppressive shadows.

The fire crackled softly, its warmth doing little to dispel the unease settling over Ellie. She shifted uncomfortably, her eyes flicking between the flickering flames and the darkened treeline.

Connor leaned back, a smug grin on his face. "You worry too much, Ellie. It's probably just squirrels or something."

Ellie didn't answer, her ears straining for any sound of movement. The stillness of the forest pressed down on her like a heavy blanket, and she couldn't shake the feeling that they weren't alone.

Ryan and Megan crept cautiously through the forest, the beam of their flashlight slicing through the darkness. Every step was accompanied by the crunch of dry leaves and the occasional snap of a twig. The air grew colder, carrying a damp, earthy scent.

Megan giggled nervously, nudging Ryan. "You hear that? Sounds like Jake's doing his best Bigfoot impression."

Ryan smirked, lowering his voice to a playful growl. "Maybe he's not Jake anymore. Maybe the forest turned him into one of those cryptids you're always scared of."

Megan slapped his arm, rolling her eyes. "Very funny. Let's just find him and get back before Ellie has a heart attack."

As they approached a gentle rise in the terrain, the noises ahead grew stranger. A soft snapping sound, almost rhythmic, echoed in the still air, followed by a hollow thud, as though something heavy was striking a tree.

Megan shivered, clutching Ryan's sleeve. "Okay, what is that? He can't be making all that noise, right?"

Ryan brushed off her concern with a confident grin. "It's probably just him kicking around to freak us out. Classic Jake. Here's the plan." He pointed toward the left side of the hill. "You loop around that way and distract him. I'll sneak up from behind and give him the scare of his life."

Megan hesitated, glancing into the shadows. "Are you sure we shouldn't just call him out and head back? This feels… off."

Ryan gave her shoulder a reassuring squeeze. "It'll be fine. It's just Jake. Trust me."

With a reluctant nod, Megan exhaled. "Alright, but don't leave me hanging if I get lost."

"Never," Ryan replied with a wink.

The forest quickly swallowed Megan's footsteps as she moved cautiously toward the source of the sounds. The rustling ahead grew louder, mingling with a wet, tearing noise that made her stomach churn. Her flashlight trembled in her grip as she approached the edge of a clearing.

The beam of light landed on a dark, hunched shape silhouetted against the faint moonlight. It moved with unnatural jerks, its shoulders heaving as it worked at something on the ground.

Megan squinted, her breath catching in her throat. It wasn't until her gaze fell lower that she realized what the shape was crouched over—Jake. Or what was left of him. His body lay twisted unnaturally, one leg mangled and torn at the joint, his chest flayed open to expose shattered ribs.

Her flashlight flickered across the surrounding trees, revealing streaks of blood splattered across the bark. Shreds of Jake's flannel shirt hung like grotesque decorations, fluttering in the cold wind.

Megan stumbled backward, her heel catching on something soft. She glanced down, the beam of her flashlight shaking as it illuminated a severed arm. The ring on its finger gleamed faintly, unmistakably Jake's.

A low, guttural growl rumbled behind her, hot breath brushing the back of her neck. Megan froze, every nerve in her body screaming at her to run, but fear held her in place.

Slowly, as though terrified of what she might see, Megan tilted her head upward. Blood dripped steadily onto her cheek, warm and sticky. Her gaze climbed higher, landing on two glowing, blood-red eyes staring down at her.

The creature loomed above, its massive frame blending into the darkness. Its jagged, blood-stained teeth glinted in the faint light, twisted into a cruel grin.

Megan's scream tore through the night, raw and primal, as she stumbled backward and fell hard onto the forest floor.

Ryan's cautious steps faltered as Megan's scream pierced the air, sending a cold shiver down his spine. He froze, the flashlight trembling in his grasp.

"Megan!" he called, his voice laced with unease. His hands clenched into fists as he took a shaky step forward.

“Megan, this isn’t funny anymore!” Ryan’s voice cracked, the oppressive silence of the forest swallowing his words.

The faint sound of snapping branches and Megan’s sobs drew him closer, but the unease in his chest grew heavier. What had started as a prank was spiraling into something far darker.

The forest seemed to tighten around him, every shadow stretching closer as if to consume him. Ryan crested a small rise, and his flashlight beam landed on a figure sprawled on the ground.

What he saw next froze him in place.

Shadows in the Fire - Part 3

In the dim light, Ryan froze as his flashlight beam fell on Megan's crumpled form. Her bright jacket, once vibrant, was now a shredded mess soaked in blood. Above her loomed a monstrous figure, its hulking body arched with sinewy muscles rippling beneath a coat of black, matted fur. The faint moonlight glinted off its grotesque muzzle, dripping with gore, and its eyes—those terrible eyes—glowed a haunting, malevolent red.

Megan's hand weakly lifted, trembling as she reached out. "Ryan... please... help me..." she whispered, her voice cracked and barely audible.

Ryan's legs locked in place, every instinct in his body screaming for him to run. But his heart wrenched at the sight of Megan, his terror mingling with guilt. The creature's gaze shifted, blood dripping from its maw as it turned to him, its fiery eyes narrowing with cold, deliberate malice.

"No... no, no, no..." Ryan whispered, his voice trembling as panic took hold. His breaths came shallow and rapid, his feet glued to the forest floor. The creature's grin widened, an unnervingly human expression, taunting him with its malevolence. It tilted its head, mocking his frozen fear.

Rising to its full height, the beast towered over Megan, its massive frame casting an oppressive shadow. Standing on its hind legs, its distorted features became even more horrifying, a perversion of both man and beast. Its clawed hand moved with deliberate cruelty, pinning Megan to the ground as her screams turned ragged and desperate.

"Leave her alone! Please!" Ryan begged, his voice cracking. But the creature's focus never wavered. Instead, it pressed its hind foot down on Megan's head, the sickening sound of cracking bones reverberating through the air.

"No! Stop!" Ryan shouted, but his body betrayed him, paralyzed by terror. He could only watch as the creature dragged its claws across Megan's face, disfiguring her with merciless precision. One of her eyes hung grotesquely against her cheek, blood streaming down her battered face. Her cries of "It hurts!" grew faint, her voice hoarse and fading.

The creature shifted, its claws slicing into her abdomen with horrifying ease. Ryan's stomach churned as her insides spilled out, glistening ribbons of gore pooling on the ground. Megan's body convulsed in its final moments, her survival instinct fighting against the inevitable.

"No, no, no…" Ryan chanted under his breath, shaking his head in disbelief. The creature raised its foot again, crushing her shattered skull with a sickening crunch. Blood sprayed across the forest floor, painting the nearby trees in crimson streaks. Megan's body went limp, her final tremors fading into stillness.

Ryan fell to his knees, sobbing uncontrollably. He stared at the lifeless remains of the girl he loved, his tears mingling with the bile rising in his throat. The creature's glowing eyes locked onto him, its grin widening as though relishing his despair. It didn't just want to kill—it wanted him to suffer.

Adrenaline surged through Ryan, propelling him to his feet. He turned to run, but a massive clawed hand swiped him from behind, hurling him against a tree. The impact knocked the air from his lungs, pain radiating through his chest as he crumpled to the ground.

Gasping for breath, Ryan tried to crawl away, but his legs buckled beneath him. Blood pooled beneath his broken body, the sticky warmth soaking into the earth. The creature loomed above, an unstoppable shadow of terror. Ryan whimpered as its claws raked across his back, tearing through flesh and muscle with sickening ease.

He couldn't feel his legs anymore, only the numbness of his impending end. As his vision blurred, the last thing he saw was the creature's fiery red eyes, burning like twin embers in the night, and the cruel satisfaction in its twisted grin.

Time seemed to stretch endlessly around the crackling fire. Connor sat lazily, a beer dangling from his hand, his posture relaxed but his movements slightly swaying from the alcohol. Across from him, Ellie sat with her knees drawn to her chest, her arms tightly wrapped around them. The flickering flames cast shadows on her pale, tense face as her wide eyes darted around the encroaching darkness.

"It's too quiet," Ellie murmured, her voice barely above a whisper. Her fingers gripped the fabric of her jeans. "Where did they go? Why haven't they come back yet?"

Connor chuckled, the sound rough and unsteady. "They're probably hiding, trying to scare us. Classic Ryan move." He smirked, taking another sip. "Don't fall for it, Ellie."

Ellie's unease deepened with every passing second. "It's not funny," she said, her voice cracking. "What if… what if something's wrong?"

Connor rolled his eyes, groaning as he pushed himself up. "Fine. You want me to play hero and go look for them? Or do you want to go?" He wobbled slightly, gesturing toward the black void beyond the firelight.

"No," Ellie stammered, shaking her head. "I… just… something's not right, Connor. I can feel it."

"Yeah, yeah. A sixth sense or whatever," Connor slurred dismissively, pulling out his phone. "I'll show you. They're just screwing around, being assholes. Watch this." He activated the camera, switching on the flashlight. The bright beam cut into the oppressive darkness. "This'll be great to rub in their faces tomorrow."

Ellie watched as he stumbled away from the fire, the light bouncing erratically with his uneven steps. The crunch of his boots against the forest floor echoed unnaturally loud in the silence. The gnawing dread in her gut intensified as the firelight shrank behind him.

The forest seemed to close in around Connor, the air growing heavier with each step. A faint, sickly odor hit his nostrils, making him wince. "What the hell?" he muttered, covering his nose.

He pressed on, muttering under his breath. "Damn Ryan and his stupid pranks." His flashlight flickered over the uneven ground, illuminating tangled roots and fallen branches. He stepped forward, only to feel something soft and squishy beneath his boot.

"What the—?" Connor jumped back, his heart hammering. "Get it together, man," he mumbled nervously. "Probably just some gross forest crap."

Curiosity got the better of him. Angling his phone downward, he shone the light on the ground. The beam illuminated a glint of metal—a thin, delicate band. Frowning, he bent down and picked it up. The object was cold and sticky in his hand. His breath caught in his throat when he realized what he was holding: a severed finger, the ring unmistakably Megan's.

"No way," Connor whispered, his voice trembling. Staggering back, the world around him seemed to spin. A low, guttural rumble sounded ahead, freezing him in place.

Slowly, Connor raised his phone, pointing the light toward the source of the sound. Two glowing red eyes pierced the darkness, unblinking and unwavering. They locked onto him from the top of a nearby hill, their intensity paralyzing him.

The creature's massive form shifted, moving with deliberate slowness. The faint outline of its towering frame grew clearer—a hulking shadow, its muscles rippling beneath dark, matted fur. It moved closer, each step purposeful, almost taunting.

"No… no, no, no!" Connor stammered, his legs finally obeying him. He turned, stumbling and tripping over roots as he sprinted back toward the fire. Connor's grip on the phone faltered for a moment, but he held on, the device still capturing the sound of his ragged breaths and frantic footsteps. Behind him, the low rumble deepened into a terrifying growl.

“Ellie!” Connor screamed, his voice raw with terror. “Ellie, run!”

The forest seemed alive, every shadow closing in, every branch reaching for him. The firelight came into view, a flickering beacon of hope in the consuming darkness. Connor didn’t stop, didn’t look back.

Ellie stood abruptly, her pulse thundering in her ears. Connor’s scream pierced the night, distant but unmistakable, sending a chill racing down her spine.

What’s happening? Are they trying to scare me? Her thoughts spiraled as dread took hold.

Shadows in the Fire - Part 4

Unable to shake the feeling of being watched, Ellie grabbed her backpack and slung it over her shoulder. The weight of her belongings offered little comfort, but at least it was something to cling to. She took a shaky step toward the path leading back to the fence.

Her footsteps crunched against the underbrush, the sound deafening in the utter stillness. Every few steps, she glanced behind her, half-expecting to see Connor stumbling out of the darkness, grinning like an idiot at her fear. But no one appeared.

By the time she reached the reserve ranger's abandoned jeep, parked crookedly near a worn dirt path, her chest felt like it might collapse from the tension. She stopped, leaning against the cool metal of the vehicle, trying to catch her breath.

That's when Connor came barreling out of the darkness.

He crashed into her, sending her sprawling to the ground with a surprised yelp. The impact knocked the wind out of her, and she scrambled to push him off.

"What the hell, Connor?!" she shouted, her voice shrill and shaking. "Not only are you trying to scare me all night, but now you're knocking me down too?"

Connor didn't answer. He crouched behind the jeep, his whole body trembling. His eyes were wide and unfocused, and his pale face glistened with sweat. His chest heaved as though he'd just run a marathon.

Ellie froze, anger momentarily forgotten. Something about his demeanor made her throat tighten.

"Connor… what's going on?" she asked, her voice softer now.

Connor fumbled with his phone, the glare of its flashlight still shining, making him seem even more frantic as he desperately tried to turn it off. He cursed under his breath, but his trembling fingers refused to cooperate.

"Connor!" Ellie snapped, grabbing his arm. "What's wrong? Where's Megan? Where's Ryan?"

His lips quivered as he tried to form words. "It's… it's out there…" he stammered, barely above a whisper.

"What's out there? What are you talking about?" Her voice trembled as her own fear began to seep through.

Connor finally looked at her, his eyes brimming with tears. "It got them," he said hoarsely. "It got them, Ellie."

Her stomach dropped, and a cold sweat broke out along her back. "What are you saying?" she whispered, dread curling around her heart.

Before he could answer, a low crack resounded from the direction of the campfire. Both of them whipped their heads toward the sound. The underbrush shuddered, as though something massive was moving through it.

The earth beneath them vibrated, a rhythmic thud, thud that grew heavier with each step. Ellie's eyes darted to Connor, who was now silently crying, his lips moving as though praying.

"What is it?" she whispered urgently.

His response came out as a barely audible croak: "It's in the trees. It can move through the trees."

Another loud crack echoed, this time closer. Ellie instinctively crouched lower, pressing herself against the jeep. The metallic surface was cold against her back, but the fear coursing through her veins burned hot.

Something heavy landed near the campfire, its weight causing a resounding thump that made the ground beneath them quiver. The faint glow of the dying fire illuminated only the edges of the thing, but its shadow seemed to stretch endlessly, consuming the light.

Ellie's breath hitched as she grabbed Connor's sleeve, pulling him closer. "What is it?!" she hissed, tears pooling in her own eyes now.

"I… I don't know," he stammered. "But it's big. And it's not human."

Another deep crack sounded, and the air filled with the pungent smell of decaying flesh, making Ellie gag. Connor buried his face in his hands, unable to look.

The two huddled together in silence, every nerve in their bodies screaming for them to run, but they didn't dare move.

A low growl emanated from the direction of the campfire, deep and guttural, reverberating in their chests. It wasn't just a sound—it was a sensation, a paralyzing force that seemed to pin them in place.

Connor's phone, still shining its flashlight, was the only thing between them and the all-consuming darkness. The realization hit Ellie like a slap.

"It can see the light," she whispered, her voice trembling with panic. "Turn it off, Connor. Turn it off now!"

Connor fumbled with the phone, his hands shaking so violently that it almost slipped from his grip. The growl intensified, moving closer, the sound of heavy footsteps crushing the underbrush around them. Connor barely managed to switch off the light, plunging them into suffocating darkness.

For a brief moment, there was silence—no growls, no movement, only the oppressive stillness of the forest. Then came the breathing, deep and deliberate, from the campfire's direction.

"It's… still there," Ellie whispered, clutching Connor's arm so tightly he could feel her nails digging into his skin.

Suddenly, the growling stopped. Connor exhaled shakily, daring to hope it had gone. But the next sound shattered that illusion—a violent crash as something massive barreled through the campfire, scattering embers into the air like fireflies.

Ellie screamed, instinct taking over as she tried to pull Connor up. “We have to run!” she cried, desperation cracking her voice.

Connor hesitated for a heartbeat too long. The creature was upon them, a shadowy blur of muscle and claws. It grabbed Connor, yanking him off his feet with terrifying ease.

“Ellie!” he screamed, his voice a raw mixture of panic and pain. “Run! Get help! Go!”

Tears streaming down her face, Ellie bolted, her legs moving on pure adrenaline. Behind her, Connor’s screams filled the air, turning guttural as the sound of ripping flesh and snapping bone echoed through the trees.

Her vision blurred with tears, Ellie stumbled and fell against the jeep, gasping for breath. The sounds of Connor’s struggle grew fainter until there was only silence.

In the clearing, Connor’s phone lay on the ground, still recording. The screen flickered as the chaos ended, and a faint, yellow text appeared:

Phantome... Hack Device... Download file... Scanning media... Asset Found!... Delete IOS.

The screen went black.

Phantome

Nathan stepped off the helicopter, the downdraft from the blades whipping up a flurry of dust and gravel around his boots. The cool evening air carried a faint metallic tang, contrasting sharply with the engine's radiant heat. Adjusting the strap of his gear bag, he scanned the landing pad with practiced precision, his sharp gaze betraying years of experience—nothing escaped him.

As his boots met solid ground, his phone vibrated against his chest, piercing the momentary calm. Fishing it out with a gloved hand, he answered without hesitation.

"This is Nathan," he said, his voice clipped, commanding.

"Nathan, we've got a situation," came the tense and urgent voice on the other end. "Something you need to see. It's... serious."

Nathan clenched his jaw, his brow furrowing. "On my way," he replied, already moving. Ending the call, he slipped the phone back into his pocket and turned to his team, who had just disembarked the helicopter and begun unloading their gear.

"Stand by," he barked, his tone sharp but steady. "No one leaves the area until I give further orders. Be ready—this sounds big."

The team exchanged knowing glances, their postures stiffening. They didn't need to ask questions; Nathan's demeanor said enough.

With purposeful strides, Nathan entered the main corridor of the base, his boots echoing faintly against the cold concrete floor. The fluorescent lights overhead cast long, sterile shadows, the hum of the bulbs a faint undertone to the tension tightening in his chest. He passed rows of cryptically labeled doors, the lifeblood of the facility pulsating around him—muffled voices, faint clatters of equipment, and the omnipresent hum of machinery.

At the end of the hall, a heavy steel door loomed. It slid open with a pneumatic hiss, revealing a room bathed in the glow of several monitors. The air inside felt heavier, as though the walls themselves carried the weight of the information within.

The Central Commander stood near the center of the room, flanked by a zoologist and an IT specialist. Their faces were pale, taut with barely concealed unease. A faint sheen of sweat glistened on the IT specialist's forehead, and the zoologist's hands were clasped tightly behind his back, his knuckles white.

"Nathan," the Commander began, his tone grave, gesturing toward the largest monitor in the room. "You need to see this. Now."

Nathan stepped closer, his sharp eyes flicking to the screen. The suffocating tension was palpable, every breath shallow, every sound amplified. His boots thudded softly against the floor as he approached, the weight of whatever awaited him pressing heavily on his shoulders.

"What am I looking at?" he asked, his voice low, steady, but edged with anticipation.

The Commander hesitated, his hand moving to a tablet to bring up a video. “We intercepted this footage. It was uploaded to a private server, but we managed to extract it before it went public.”

Nathan’s brow furrowed as the screen flickered to life. What he saw made his stomach drop—a scene of pure carnage. A shaky camera captured the agonizing screams of a young man being torn apart with horrifying precision by something massive, dark, and all too familiar.

The sound of bones snapping filled the room, and Nathan’s jaw tightened. His throat felt dry as his eyes flicked across the screen, capturing every gruesome detail. The camera’s flashlight illuminated the creature—a towering, black-furred beast with glowing red eyes. Its claws glistened with blood as it tossed its victim like a ragdoll, the screams fading into haunting silence.

Nathan’s fists clenched at his sides. “How did this happen?” he demanded, his voice cold but simmering with anger. “What the hell were they doing inside the reserve? Didn’t we lock it down?”

The Commander exchanged a glance with the zoologist before responding. “They cut through the perimeter fence. Five of them—kids. Teenagers, most likely. They thought it was all just stories to scare people off.”

Nathan’s scowl deepened. “And now?”

The IT specialist spoke up, his voice trembling slightly. “We’ve confirmed one fatality from the video. But the rest… we don’t know yet. They could all be dead.”

Nathan let out a slow, measured breath, his gaze fixed on the screen. "If they're not, they're as good as," he muttered.

The zoologist cleared his throat nervously. "If there's any chance someone survived, they won't be far. You know how it works, Nathan."

Nathan turned his piercing gaze on him, then back to the Commander. "So what do you need from me?"

The Commander straightened. "We need that phone. The one that recorded this." He gestured to the screen, where the creature now loomed over its lifeless prey, breathing heavily, its red eyes almost taunting the camera. "There's data on that phone we can't risk anyone else finding."

Nathan's eyes narrowed. "I thought you said you wiped the footage."

The IT specialist spoke quickly, "We did—everything stored on the phone's internal drive. But if anything was backed up to a SIM card or external server, it's a problem. We can't take that risk."

Nathan exhaled sharply, his patience thinning. "What's the mission, exactly?"

The Commander leaned forward. "Recover the phone. Retrieve the SIM card. Secure the area. And if there's anyone still alive out there, they're coming back with you. Understood?"

Nathan nodded curtly. "Understood."

Nathan strode purposefully into the team briefing room, his boots echoing against the cold, metallic floor. The room was sparsely lit, a tactical map glowing faintly on a central display. Around the table, his team stood, their eyes snapping to attention as he entered.

"Alright, listen up," Nathan began, his voice calm but laced with urgency. "We've got a serious problem to solve."

The men and women stiffened, the weight of his words settling over the room like a heavy fog. Nathan paced slowly, each step deliberate, as the tension mounted.

"Helmets on," he ordered, gesturing toward the lockers along the wall. The team immediately complied, the sound of clasps snapping into place punctuating the otherwise silent room. "IT, send the video feed to the main screen. Everyone needs to see what we're walking into."

The screen flickered to life, and the room darkened as the footage began to play. Grainy, shaky camera work. Heavy breathing. Then the screams. Horrifying, gut-wrenching screams. The grotesque scene unfolded in brutal clarity—an unrelenting display of terror and savagery. The sound of flesh tearing, bones snapping, and desperate pleas echoed through the room.

One of the newer recruits, pale as a ghost, muttered, "This is… this is messed up. I mean, what the hell is that thing?"

Nathan's head whipped around, his sharp gaze pinning the recruit in place. "Enough!" he barked, his voice cutting through the air like a blade. “This is what happens if we don’t stick together, if we slip up. That thing is smarter than you think. It knows how to manipulate, how to make you panic. And panic kills.”

His words hung in the air, every syllable heavy with warning.

“But we don’t panic,” Nathan continued, his voice rising with conviction. “Because we are—what?”

“PHANTOME!” the team shouted in unison, the sound reverberating off the steel walls like a war cry.

“That’s right,” Nathan said, his tone hard as iron. “We don’t make mistakes. Pack your weapons, ammo, and bring the HOWLERS. We’re also taking the ultrasound equipment—low-frequency sound waves will mess with its equilibrium, thanks to its K9 genetics. Every edge counts.”

The team scrambled into action, grabbing gear from their lockers and checking their equipment with the precision of a well-oiled machine. Nathan moved between them, his hands briefly clapping each on the shoulder or back as they passed. It was more than a gesture of encouragement—it was a ritual, a bond forged in trust and battle.

Outside, the helicopter blades were already spinning, their rhythmic thrum growing louder as the team approached. Nathan adjusted his own gear, snapping his helmet into place. The emblem—a snarling wolf flanked by crossed swords—gleamed in the dim light.

The hunt was on.

The Hunt - Part 1

As they climbed into the helicopter, the team settled into their seats, their faces illuminated by the faint glow of their HUD displays. Nathan stood by the open door for a moment, his silhouette stark against the whirling chaos of the rotors. He turned to address his team one last time.

"Our mission is clear," he began, his voice steady despite the mounting tension. "Primary objective: retrieve the phone and the SIM card for analysis. That data cannot fall into the wrong hands. Secondary objective: if there are any survivors, we extract them. No exceptions. And if the mutt shows up—" Nathan paused, his eyes scanning each face. "—we're ready."

"YES, SIR!" the team roared back, their collective energy vibrating through the cabin.

The helicopter lifted off, slicing through the night sky. Nathan strapped himself in, his eyes fixed on the distant horizon. His team was prepared, but he knew better than anyone that the Alpha was never predictable. This was no ordinary mission—it was a hunt, and they were stepping into the predator's territory.

The steady thrum of the helicopter blades sliced through the night air as it descended toward the clearing. The rotors kicked up a whirlwind of dust and debris, swirling around the Phantom team as they crouched low, shielding their faces. Nathan stood at the open door, his boots braced against the floor, his sharp eyes scanning the dense forest surrounding the drop zone.

"This is it," he muttered, hooking himself to the rappelling line. His voice cut through the comms in his team's helmets. "We hit the ground, we move. No hesitation."

The team's acknowledgments came swiftly, their voices calm and focused. Nathan tugged at the line to ensure its stability before stepping out, descending rapidly into the shadows below. He landed with a solid thud, the gravel crunching beneath his boots. He unclipped the harness and waved for the next operative to follow.

One by one, the team dropped into formation, their landings reverberating softly in the unnerving stillness of the forest. The only sound was the faint hum of the helicopter overhead, which quickly faded as it lifted off, leaving them surrounded by an oppressive silence.

Nathan turned, his sharp gaze meeting the eyes of his team through their visors. "We've got a bit of ground to cover before we hit the fence where the breach occurred. Stay low, stay quiet. We move in a V formation, and I want eyes everywhere."

The operatives nodded in unison, falling into position with precision. Nathan took point, his steps calculated and nearly soundless against the damp earth. The forest closed in around them, the skeletal branches of trees stretching like claws overhead, blotting out the faint moonlight.

They moved as shadows through the terrain, the whisper of leaves underfoot the only indication of their passage. The air was thick with the scent of damp foliage and decay, and every rustle of leaves seemed amplified in the suffocating quiet.

Nathan raised his fist abruptly, bringing the formation to a halt. The team froze, rifles raised, their trained eyes scanning the darkness for any signs of movement. The forest seemed alive with menace, every shadow holding a potential threat.

Nathan pressed a button on his wrist-mounted interface, activating his night vision. The forest lit up in shades of green, the barren landscape stretching endlessly ahead. His team followed suit, the faint hum of their night-vision devices the only sound breaking the silence.

"Bingo," Nathan murmured, his gaze locking onto a dark shape ahead. It was the car. The one that had belonged to the teenagers.

"Central," he said into his comms, his voice barely above a whisper. "We've located the vehicle. Advancing to investigate."

He motioned for the team to follow, and they moved as one, their steps ghostly quiet. The car sat eerily still, its windows fogged over from the humid night air. Nathan approached it cautiously, his weapon drawn. He leaned in to peer through the window, his eyes scanning the interior.

"Vehicle's empty," he reported. "No signs of movement. Looks like it's been here for hours."

"Copy that," Central responded. "Continue the search. Coordinates for the phone's last known location are being uploaded now."

Nathan stepped back from the car and turned to his team. "We've got tracks," one of them said, gesturing to the soft earth nearby. Nathan crouched beside the marks, his gloved fingers brushing against the indentations. Five sets of footprints, leading toward the forest.

"They went that way," Nathan confirmed, rising to his full height. "Looks like they moved toward the fence about 100 meters in."

He turned to his team, his tone shifting to a sharper edge. "Alright, listen up. This is no longer a search-and-rescue. This is live ops. Load sharp ammo and activate HOWLER."

One of the operatives dropped to a knee, pulling a small drone from their pack. They placed it carefully on the ground, and Nathan tapped his wrist device. The drone whirred to life, lifting silently into the air, its sensors scanning the surroundings.

"If it picks up anything—movement, bodies, or anything not human—we'll get a ping," Nathan said. "Let's move."

The team advanced toward the tree line, weapons raised, every step deliberate and measured. When they reached the fence, Nathan signaled for a halt. The breach loomed ahead—a jagged hole in the chain-link, its edges frayed and curling outward like sharp talons.

"Goddamn kids," Nathan muttered under his breath as he examined the damage. "What the hell did you get yourselves into?"

He straightened, gesturing to the opening. "Two-man breach," he ordered. "Cover angles. We don't know what's waiting on the other side."

Two operatives slipped through the hole, rifles sweeping the immediate area. They signaled the all-clear, and the rest of the team followed, moving swiftly but silently. Nathan was the last to cross, his eyes lingering on the torn fence as a gnawing unease settled in his chest.

Once inside, Nathan tapped his wrist device again. "Central, HOWLER is airborne. I need the exact coordinates for the phone."

A waypoint flashed on his HUD, a small icon pulsing against the digital map overlay. "Coordinates locked," Central responded. "1.5 kilometers northeast. Proceed with caution."

Nathan turned to his team, his voice steady but firm. "We've got a kilometer and a half to cover. Eyes open, and report any movement, no matter how small. Stay sharp."

The team moved in unison, their silhouettes melting into the shadows of the forest. The hum of the HOWLER drone overhead was a constant reminder of their mission's urgency. Nathan's grip tightened on his rifle as they pressed deeper into the unknown, the oppressive weight of the forest bearing down on them.

The Hunt - Part 2

The faint beep from the HOWLER broke the tense silence, its rhythmic pulse sending an icy shiver through the team. Nathan's hand shot up, signaling the group to halt. They dropped low into a crouch, weapons raised, forming a protective circle around the source of the alert. Nathan's HUD flickered as he brought up the drone's feed. His jaw clenched at the grainy image that appeared—a figure lying prone among the underbrush.

"HOWLER's picked something up," Nathan muttered into his comms, his voice low but firm. He adjusted the angle of the feed, trying to sharpen the image. The figure was human. Female.

"It looks like one of them."

"Status?" Central's voice crackled through the earpiece.

Nathan hesitated, his eyes narrowing as he studied the still form on his display. "Unknown," he replied. "Moving in to confirm. Hold tight for updates."

With a quick gesture, Nathan motioned for the team to advance. They moved in synchrony, their boots barely making a sound against the damp earth. The forest loomed larger with every step, the oppressive darkness swallowing them whole. Nathan's grip tightened on his rifle as they closed in on the location.

The girl came into view, her body sprawled in a heap, pale and motionless. Nathan signaled a halt, and the team spread out, taking defensive positions in a wide arc around the area.

"Eyes up," Nathan commanded, his voice sharp. "If this is a trap, it's a good one."

The tension was palpable as Nathan approached the girl, his every movement calculated and deliberate. He knelt beside her, the barrel of his rifle still trained on the surrounding shadows. Her face was ghastly pale, her lips tinged blue. She looked almost frozen, a fragile doll abandoned in the wilderness.

"Central," Nathan whispered. "We've got a survivor. I think."

The girl's body shuddered suddenly, her limbs jerking as if awakened from a nightmare. Her eyes flew open, bloodshot and wild, and a piercing scream tore through the air. The sound was raw and primal, a visceral cry that echoed off the trees and sent chills down the team's spines.

"Shit," one of the soldiers muttered, his rifle swinging toward the noise. The team pivoted instinctively, scanning the forest for movement.

Nathan removed his helmet, setting it aside as he crouched lower, his sharp features softening as he met the girl's terrified gaze. Her pupils were dilated, her breath coming in ragged gasps, and her hands trembled uncontrollably.

"Hey, hey, it's okay," Nathan said, his tone firm but calm. "You're safe now. Look at me."

Her eyes darted frantically around the clearing, her lips quivering as she tried to form words. "It's… it's everywhere," she stammered, her voice barely a whisper. "It's watching…"

Nathan's stomach twisted at her words. He glanced back at his team. "Stay sharp!" he barked, his voice slicing through the tension. "Cover the perimeter. This could be bait."

Returning his focus to the girl, he softened his tone. "What's your name?" he asked, trying to ground her in the moment. "Can you tell me your name?"

She blinked rapidly, her chest heaving as she fought to control her breathing. "E-Ellie," she managed to choke out, her voice breaking.

"Ellie," Nathan repeated, nodding. "Good. That's good. Ellie, I need you to tell me how many of you there were. Can you do that?"

Tears spilled down her cheeks as she began to sob, her body shaking with the force of it. "Five," she finally gasped. "There were five of us… but they… they didn't listen. I told them. I told them we shouldn't come here!"

Her voice cracked as she dissolved into a fit of tears. Nathan reached out, gently placing a hand on her shoulder. Her skin was icy to the touch, her body wracked with shivers. He turned his head toward the team. "Jennie!" he called, his voice urgent.

One of the female operatives sprinted forward, unslinging her pack as she knelt beside Nathan. Without hesitation, she pulled out a thermal jacket and draped it over Ellie's trembling form.

"Here," Jennie said softly, fastening the jacket around Ellie's shoulders. She met Nathan's eyes and gave a curt nod before retreating to her position, weapon raised and ready.

Nathan adjusted the jacket, making sure it fit snugly. "Ellie," he said, keeping his voice steady. "Listen to me. You're safe now. But I need you to stay with me, okay?"

Ellie nodded weakly, her tear-streaked face turning toward him. "It's still out there," she whispered, her voice filled with dread. "It's watching us… waiting…"

Nathan felt the weight of her words settle over him like a lead blanket. His gut told him she wasn't wrong. He scanned the darkness, the forest seeming to pulse with an unseen life. The predator was near. He could feel it.

"Stay ready," he said to the team, his voice tight. "Whatever's out there, it won't catch us off guard."

The Hunt - Part 3

Nathan took a deep breath, steadying himself against the torrent of emotions Ellie was unleashing. Her sobs were raw and unfiltered, the kind of despair that cut deeper than fear—it was the crushing realization of loss. He crouched in front of her, leveling his gaze with hers, his voice calm but firm.

"Ellie, I need you to listen to me carefully," he said, his tone softening slightly but never losing its edge. "Is there anyone else alive? Anyone who might have made it?"

Ellie sniffled, her shoulders trembling as she fought to compose herself. "I—I don't think so," she whimpered, shaking her head. "It came out of nowhere… it just… it took them, one by one. I couldn't do anything…" Her voice cracked, and fresh tears spilled down her cheeks. Nathan could feel the weight of her anguish pressing down on the moment, a suffocating tension that gripped the air around them.

Nathan placed a steadying hand on her shoulder. Her frailty was evident, her skin icy to the touch, and her lips trembled as though the mere act of speaking was draining what little energy she had left. "Ellie," he said, his voice firmer now, "I understand how you feel. But you need to help us. We have to find where this happened."

Her eyes widened in terror, and she instinctively pulled back, shaking her head violently. "No!" she cried, her words coming out in stuttering gasps. "I don't want to go back there! I can't! I just want to go home! Please, I don't want to be here anymore!"

Nathan leaned closer, gripping her gently but firmly by the shoulders. His voice dropped to a serious tone that left no room for argument. “Ellie, look at me.” She hesitated, her bloodshot eyes meeting his. “We’re your only way out of here. If you don’t work with us, if you panic, if you make any sudden moves, no one will get out alive. Do you understand me?”

Her lips quivered as she nodded shakily, the tears continuing to flow down her face. “I just want to go home,” she whimpered. “I didn’t even want to come here! I told them… I told them it was a bad idea, but no one listened! Now they’re all gone!”

Nathan exhaled, his jaw tightening as he processed her words. “Which direction were you?” he asked, his tone softening slightly, though his focus remained sharp. “Where did it happen?”

Ellie raised a trembling hand and pointed into the dense blackness of the forest. The darkness seemed to pulse, almost alive, devouring the light as though daring them to follow. Nathan’s gut tightened, but his expression remained unreadable. He couldn’t afford to let her see his unease.

“You’re strong, Ellie,” Nathan said, his voice steady and low. “You’ve made it this far. That’s no small thing—you’ve had more luck than most.”

Ellie’s tear-streaked face turned toward him, her expression shifting into one of faint recognition. “You… you know what it is, don’t you?” she asked, her voice barely above a whisper. Her gaze flickered to the other soldiers, her fear evident. "You all know."

Nathan straightened slightly, his lips pressing into a thin line. He exhaled through his nose, the weight of her question heavy in the still air. "I know more than I'd like to," he admitted, his tone laced with grim resolve. "But right now, that's not the problem. I need to know something, Ellie. One of you had a phone, didn't you? You were filming, weren't you?"

Ellie hesitated, her lips parting as if to speak but unable to form the words. Finally, she nodded. "Connor," she stammered. "Connor had the phone."

Nathan's eyes narrowed. "Do you know where it is?" he pressed. "I have to find it, Ellie. It's critical."

Ellie swallowed hard, her voice barely audible as she replied. "Connor… he still had it when… when the darkness took him. He told me to run… to get help." Her voice broke again, and she dissolved into quiet sobs.

Nathan clenched his jaw, glancing back at his team, who remained vigilant in their defensive positions. His mind raced. The phone was likely still on Connor—assuming there was anything left of him to find. It was a grim reality he couldn't shield Ellie from, no matter how much he wanted to.

"Ellie," he said, his voice calm but unyielding, "I know this is hard, but we need to move. You're coming with us. We'll get you out of here, I promise, but we need that phone—and we need to know exactly where you were. Can you do that?"

She nodded hesitantly, wiping at her face with trembling hands. Nathan stood, signaling to Jennie. "Stay close to her," he ordered, his tone clipped. "Keep her calm. We can't afford to lose her now."

Jennie gave a sharp nod, moving to Ellie's side and offering a reassuring presence. Nathan turned back to the team, his voice cutting through the stillness. "Gear up. We're moving out. Stay sharp, eyes on the perimeter. Whatever's out there, it's not going to catch us off guard."

The forest swallowed them as they moved deeper into its shadowy embrace, every step muffled by the damp moss carpeting the ground. The air was thick and stifling, carrying an unnatural stillness that seemed to press down on them. Ellie stumbled slightly, Jennie's firm hand catching her arm before she could fall.

"Stay close," Jennie whispered, her voice steady but low. "You're doing fine, Ellie. Just breathe."

Ellie nodded weakly, her breaths shallow and erratic. Her eyes darted around the encroaching darkness, every flicker of movement at the edge of her vision sending fresh waves of dread coursing through her body.

A faint rustling came from somewhere ahead, followed by a low, drawn-out creak. Ellie froze mid-step, her grip tightening on Jennie's arm.

"Did you hear that?" she whispered, her voice trembling.

Jennie glanced toward the sound but saw nothing. "It's just the wind," she murmured, trying to sound reassuring. "Keep moving."

Ellie didn't reply, her eyes fixed on the dense undergrowth. A pair of shadows shifted against the trees, too quick to focus on, and her heart began to race.

Nathan paused, raising a clenched fist to signal a halt. The group stopped instantly, their eyes scanning the darkness. "Report," he whispered into his comms, his tone sharp.

No response came, only the sound of Ellie's ragged breathing. Jennie leaned in closer. "Ellie, we need to keep going," she urged softly. "We're almost there."

But Ellie wasn't listening. Her gaze was locked on the void between the trees. She swore she could see eyes staring back at her, faint and glowing like embers. She tugged on Jennie's arm. "It's watching us," she hissed, her voice breaking. "I can feel it."

Jennie turned to Nathan, her voice firm. "She's losing it. We need to calm her down, or we're not getting anywhere."

Nathan glanced back at them, his expression hard but not unkind. He approached Ellie slowly, crouching slightly to meet her eyes. "Ellie, look at me," he said, his voice steady. "You're safe as long as you're with us. Whatever's out there, we're going to handle it. But I need you to focus. Can you do that for me?"

Ellie nodded shakily, her tears glinting in the faint moonlight. “It’s so dark,” she whispered. “It’s everywhere.”

Nathan placed a reassuring hand on her shoulder, his voice softening. “Stay close to Jennie and keep moving. We’ll get out of this.”

Another sound broke through the stillness—a deep, hollow groan that seemed to emanate from the trees themselves. Ellie flinched, her body trembling as the sound reverberated through the forest.

“Eyes up,” Nathan ordered, his voice cutting through the rising tension. “It’s close.”

The Hunt - Part 4

As they pressed forward, the air grew heavier, the metallic tang of blood thickening with every step. Ellie's stomach churned as a putrid smell assaulted her senses. She gagged, covering her mouth and nose as tears streamed down her face.

Then they saw it.

The remnants of her friends lay scattered across a small clearing. Blood soaked the earth, pooling around torn limbs and shredded clothing. Ellie froze, her knees buckling before she crumpled to the ground, her body convulsing with dry heaves.

Jennie was beside her in an instant, pulling her into an embrace and shielding her face from the grisly scene. "Don't look," Jennie whispered, her tone firm yet soothing. "Just breathe. Focus on me."

Nathan moved forward cautiously, his face grim as his sharp eyes scanned the horrific tableau. He crouched low, his gaze snagging on a blood-smeared object partially hidden beneath a tangle of foliage. Gritting his teeth, he reached for it and pulled out a phone—its screen cracked, but miraculously intact.

"Found it," Nathan muttered, holding it up for the team to see. The momentary relief in his tone was fleeting.

Ellie's muffled sobs broke through the heavy silence. "We have to leave!" she cried, her voice laced with hysteria. "It's still here! It's going to kill us!"

Nathan turned to her, his tone calm but resolute. "Ellie, listen to me. I need you to focus. Tell me exactly what happened. Did you see the attack? Anything that can help us understand this thing?"

Ellie shook her head violently, fresh tears streaming down her face. "It came out of nowhere," she stammered, her breathing ragged. "We didn't hear it... until it was too late."

Nathan pressed further, his gaze unwavering. "From where, Ellie? From the ground?"

Her eyes darted toward the treetops, a memory surfacing with painful clarity. "No," she whispered, her voice trembling. "It came from above. From the trees."

Nathan froze, his sharp instincts bristling. "The trees?" he repeated, his voice dropping into a low growl. "Are you sure?"

Ellie nodded frantically. "Connor… he said it was in the trees before it jumped on him. We didn't even have time to run." Her voice broke again, dissolving into sobs.

Nathan straightened, his jaw tightening as his mind raced. He tapped his comms. "Central, do you copy?"

"Go ahead, Nathan," came the reply, the static-laden voice steady.

Nathan's tone was clipped, his words charged with tension. "We've got a bigger problem. The target isn't just on the ground. It's using the trees. Repeat—it's climbing and attacking from above."

A brief silence followed before Central responded, their voice betraying unease. "Understood. Adjusting protocol."

Nathan turned back to his team, his expression grim. "Eyes up," he ordered, his voice sharp and commanding. "We're not just dealing with ground-level attacks anymore."

He crouched in front of Ellie, his tone softening as he addressed her. "You did good, Ellie. You gave us what we needed. Just hold on a little longer."

Jennie helped Ellie to her feet, keeping a firm grip on her arm. Nathan took one last look at the grotesque scene, his stomach twisting at the carnage. "Let's move," he said firmly. "And stay alert. This thing isn't done yet."

Nathan lowered his voice as the team regrouped, his words cutting through the oppressive silence. "Switch off your safeties. It's just us out here. If anything moves—if anything shows itself—free fire. Understood?"

The team nodded in unison, their safeties clicking off with quiet finality. Nathan inhaled deeply, steadying himself against the pounding of his heart. "Activate paralysis rounds," he commanded. "We're not killing it with Ellie here, but we can buy ourselves enough time to get out alive."

The faint glow of red indicators lit up across their weapons, signaling the switch. Jennie moved closer to Ellie, her expression stern but reassuring. "We're getting out of here," she said in a low, steady voice. "But now you need to listen to Nathan. Exactly what he says. Otherwise, none of us are making it out. Understand?"

Ellie nodded shakily, her wide, tear-filled eyes darting between Jennie and Nathan. The fear gripping her made words impossible, but the subtle movement of her head was enough.

Nathan's wrist device glowed faintly as he tapped rapidly through the interface. A waypoint blinked to life on his HUD: "2 kilometers south. Limited lift zone. 20 minutes."

"Got it," Nathan muttered, pressing a confirmation. He turned to the team, his voice cutting through the tension. "We've got 20 minutes to cover two kilometers south. Stay in formation—ten-meter spacing. Watch every shadow."

The team fell into formation, their movements precise and disciplined. Nathan took a deep breath, his voice steady but urgent. "Send Howler up. We'll need it as our eyes."

The Hunt - Part 5

The drone whirred softly and lifted into the air, hovering three meters above their heads. Its rhythmic green light pulsed as it began scanning the area for movement, a silent guardian in the pitch-black forest.

Nathan swiped a hand across his forehead, feeling sweat bead despite the cool night air. Jennie moved closer, her voice low but firm. "Nathan," she said, her tone edged with urgency. "We need to move. Now."

Nathan nodded once, his eyes narrowing. "You and Ellie, third in the formation. Keep her calm," he instructed, his voice clipped but steady.

The group began to move, their steps precise but quick, navigating the dark terrain with trained efficiency. Ellie stuck close to Jennie, clutching her backpack as though it were the only thing anchoring her to reality.

The only sound breaking the silence was Howler's soft, constant swish above them. The forest around them felt alive, its darkness pressing in like a suffocating blanket. Even the trees seemed to lean closer, their skeletal branches barely swaying in the faint breeze high above.

Jennie glanced sideways at Ellie, who was visibly trembling. "The quiet is good," Jennie said softly, trying to soothe her. "Quiet means we still have time."

Ellie didn't respond, her gaze darting to the shifting shadows around them. She felt it—a presence, watching her from the depths of the darkness. Her breath hitched, and she whispered, "It's there… I can feel it."

Jennie tensed but didn't stop moving. "Eyes forward," she murmured. "If it shows itself, we'll handle it. Just keep walking."

Ellie nodded shakily, but her steps faltered. The further they went, the more her panic clawed at her. She could swear she saw movement at the edges of her vision—a flicker of something unnatural, too quick to pinpoint.

Nathan raised a fist abruptly, signaling the team to stop. Everyone froze, weapons raised, scanning their surroundings with laser focus. Howler's green light continued to pulse steadily, but nothing registered on its sensors. Nathan checked his wrist display. 17 minutes left.

"Keep moving," he ordered, his voice low and tense. "Stay sharp."

The team resumed their march, moving like phantoms through the dense forest. Ellie glanced at Jennie again, her voice trembling. "It's watching me," she whispered.

Jennie tightened her grip on her weapon, glancing back at Ellie. "Eyes forward. Whatever's out there won't get to you. We won't let it."

Ellie nodded again, but her breaths came faster, shallower. Her imagination twisted every shadow into something monstrous, and she could feel her resolve beginning to crack.

Nathan glanced back at Jennie and Ellie, his sharp gaze softening for a moment as he caught Jennie's subtle nod. They were holding it together —for now. But he knew their time was running out, and not just because of the ticking clock.

Jennie glanced back at Ellie, trying to keep her focused as they trudged forward. "Hey," Jennie whispered, her voice calm but steady, "how're you holding up?"

Ellie shrugged slightly, her breathing uneven. "I don't know… I just want to get out of here."

Jennie nodded, her gaze scanning the darkness. "We're close. Just stick with me, alright? Nathan knows what he's doing. We're going to make it out."

Ellie swallowed hard and nodded, her fingers clutching the straps of her backpack as if holding on to her sanity. The oppressive silence around them felt alive, each step amplifying her fear. She whispered, "It feels like it's still watching us."

Jennie didn't respond immediately, her eyes darting to the shadows. "Keep your focus," she murmured. "If it shows itself, we'll deal with it."

Ellie's steps faltered slightly. Her heart raced as her imagination turned every movement at the edges of her vision into a lurking predator. The gentle swish of Howler overhead was the only sound accompanying them, a faint reminder that they weren't entirely alone.

Suddenly, Ellie froze mid-step, her eyes wide with panic. Jennie stopped beside her, her instincts sharp. A faint, soft chime echoed from Howler—a warning ping. Jennie's hand flew up, signaling the group to halt.

Nathan's voice broke the silence, calm but commanding. "Stay alert. Eyes on the trees and the ground."

Ellie trembled, clutching Jennie's arm as she whispered, "I see it…"

Jennie crouched beside her, following Ellie's gaze. The girl's trembling finger pointed toward a tree about five meters ahead. Jennie's breath caught as her eyes locked on the faint glow of red—two piercing eyes staring down from the branches. The creature was motionless, its gaze calculating, as if planning its next move.

Jennie leaned in closer to Ellie, her voice barely audible. "Stay quiet, Ellie. Don't move."

She activated her comms with a soft tap. "Nathan," she whispered, her tone laced with urgency, "we've got a problem."

Nathan froze mid-step, turning slightly. "You see it?"

Jennie nodded, though he couldn't see her. "Forty meters ahead, five meters up in the trees."

Nathan exhaled slowly, the tension in his shoulders visible even in the dim light. His voice dropped. "Everyone, weapons ready. Aim for the target—five meters up. On my mark."

The team shifted in unison, their weapons leveling at the spot Jennie indicated. Nathan took a deep breath, his voice cutting through the silence like a blade. “Fire.”

The deafening roar of gunfire shattered the stillness. The forest exploded with sound, each shot echoing off the trees. Ellie screamed, clamping her hands over her ears as the cacophony overwhelmed her. The vibrations from the gunfire made her knees buckle, and she nearly collapsed into Jennie’s arms.

The creature moved in a blur, dropping from the tree with terrifying agility. Its massive frame was a shadowy blur as it darted through the underbrush, leaping over logs and boulders with an eerie, almost human-like precision. The team’s barrage of shots tracked it, but it was too fast.

“Cease fire!” Nathan barked, his voice sharp. The weapons fell silent, the forest eerily quiet except for the rapid breathing of the team. Then, a bone-chilling roar ripped through the night, vibrating through the ground and sending a fresh wave of terror coursing through Ellie.

She sobbed into Jennie’s chest, her body trembling violently. “It’s still here… it’s coming back,” she whimpered.

Nathan glanced back, his eyes narrowing at the sight of Jennie trying to comfort Ellie. He activated his wrist device, the countdown glowing ominously. “300 meters. Two minutes.”

The faint hum of rotor blades reached his ears, distant but growing.

Relief flickered briefly across his face, quickly replaced by grim determination. "We need to run!"

He turned to his team. "You three at the back, get moving now! Cover us from the rear once you reach the clearing."

The soldiers nodded, their movements precise and quick. Like shadows, they darted ahead into the darkness, disappearing toward the evac point. Nathan turned back to Jennie and Ellie, his voice steady but urgent. "Jennie, move! Get her up and let's go!"

Jennie nodded, pulling Ellie to her feet. Nathan grabbed Ellie's arm, his grip firm but not rough. "We run now, Ellie. Don't stop for anything. Do you hear me?"

Ellie's body shook as she nodded, her voice barely above a whisper. "I understand."

"Go!" Nathan shouted, propelling her forward.

The Hunt - Part 6

Jennie took the lead, her steps purposeful and swift, with Nathan and Ellie close behind. The new recruit brought up the rear, his eyes darting nervously through the trees. The clearing came into view, the faint glow of the helicopter's spotlight cutting through the dark. Jennie emerged first, turning back toward Nathan with a questioning look. "Where's the rookie?"

Nathan spun around, scanning the path they'd just taken. The recruit was nowhere to be seen.

A sudden, blood-curdling scream erupted from the trees, followed by the staccato burst of gunfire. Nathan clenched his jaw, his voice a low growl. "Dammit… it's too late. We have to move!"

Jennie didn't hesitate, sprinting to the waiting helicopter. She grabbed the dangling evac line and was hoisted up quickly, her weapon still clutched tightly in her hands.

Nathan turned to Ellie, his expression hard but focused. "Ellie, it's our turn. When we get there, you grab the line, and they'll pull you up. Do not stop for anything. Do you understand?"

Ellie's body shook as she nodded, her voice barely above a whisper. "I understand."

"Go!" Nathan shouted, propelling her forward.

The two sprinted toward the helicopter, its rotors kicking up a whirlwind of dust and leaves. The earth beneath their feet seemed to shake with the approach of something massive, each thudding step reverberating through their bodies. Nathan felt the vibrations in the ground intensify, each tremor signaling the approach of the beast. The sound of its heavy, labored breaths reached his ears, chilling him to the core. He tightened his grip on Ellie's arm, propelling her forward. The helicopter loomed ahead, its rotors slicing the air with urgency.

"Keep running!" Nathan barked, his voice cutting through the deafening chaos.

Ellie stumbled, her exhaustion overtaking her. "I... I can't!" she cried, her legs giving out beneath her.

Nathan didn't hesitate. He hoisted her up and onto his shoulder, his own strength beginning to waver. Every instinct screamed to move faster, but the ground quaked harder with each step, as though the beast was closing the distance with inhuman speed.

Jennie was already aboard, leaning out of the helicopter, her eyes wide with alarm as she spotted Nathan and Ellie. "Hurry! It's coming!" she screamed, her rifle trained on the treeline.

Nathan reached the evac line, placing Ellie's hands onto it. "Hold on tight, Ellie! Don't let go, no matter what!" he ordered. She clung to the rope, her small frame trembling violently.

The winch began to pull her upward, and Nathan grabbed onto the line behind her. His eyes never left the shadows of the forest, scanning for the first sign of movement. The beast's low growl echoed, sending a shiver down his spine.

Then it happened.

The creature burst from the treeline, a blur of black and crimson. It launched itself into the air with terrifying speed, its claws slashing through Ellie's leg and ripping her from the line.

"ELLIE!" Nathan roared, his voice cracking with desperation as he watched her plummet to the ground.

Ellie screamed as she hit the dirt, her voice piercing the night. The beast landed beside her, its massive body blocking Nathan's view.

Jennie fired wildly from the helicopter, her bullets finding their mark but barely slowing the creature. "Get away from her, you bastard!" she yelled, her voice raw with panic.

Ellie scrambled backward, her wide, tear-filled eyes locking with Nathan's. "Help me!" she sobbed, her voice a broken whisper as the beast's claws pinned her to the earth.

Nathan struggled against the line, his arms shaking as he tried to descend back to the ground, but the winch pulled him upward too quickly. "No, no, no!" he growled, his heart pounding in his chest.

The creature's head lowered toward Ellie, its glowing red eyes studying her as though savoring the moment. Then, with a sickening crunch, its jaws clamped onto her shoulder.

Ellie's screams turned into gurgled cries, her blood spraying across the forest floor. "Nathan! Jennie! Please!" she begged, her hands weakly batting at the monster's massive head.

Jennie's rifle clicked empty. "No!" she sobbed, her hands fumbling to reload. "She's just a kid! Nathan, do something!"

Nathan's vision blurred with rage and anguish. He raised his wrist-mounted device, locking onto the beast's massive shoulder. With a sharp hiss, the tracking beacon fired, embedding itself deep into the creature's flesh.

The beast snapped its head toward him, its blood-soaked face twisting into a grotesque snarl. Nathan pressed a second button, detonating a small charge near the beacon. The explosion sent shrapnel into the creature's side, causing it to stagger.

But it wasn't enough.

The monster turned back to Ellie, its claws raking across her abdomen. Her final scream echoed into the night as the creature tore her apart, piece by agonizing piece.

Jennie turned away, her shoulders heaving with silent sobs. "She's gone..." she whispered, her voice hollow.

Nathan was hoisted into the helicopter, his breath shallow and uneven. The beast stepped back from Ellie's mangled remains, its blood-red eyes meeting Nathan's with cold, calculated malice.

Then, it smiled—a chilling, human-like grin that sent a shiver through Nathan's entire body. Without a sound, the creature turned and disappeared into the forest, its hulking form swallowed by the darkness.

Nathan collapsed onto the floor of the helicopter, his fists clenched so tightly his nails bit into his palms. His voice was hoarse as he spoke into his comms. "Central... we have the phone."

"And the girl?" came the response.

Nathan closed his eyes, Ellie's final cries still ringing in his ears. "She didn't make it," he said flatly. "Tracker's active. It'll lead us to the target."

"Understood," Central replied. "Return to base."

Jennie sat across from him, her face pale and streaked with tears. She muttered under her breath, "She was just a child..."

Nathan didn't reply. He leaned his head back, staring blankly at the ceiling of the helicopter as it ascended into the night. The beast had won, and they both knew it.

Revenge - Part 1

The helicopter's steady thrum filled the cabin, a low vibration that seemed to seep into Nathan's very bones. Outside, the endless black of the forest stretched like a void, the faintest hints of moonlight cutting through the canopy below. The red interior lighting bathed the cabin in an ominous glow, deepening the shadows under Nathan's eyes.

In his gloved hand, Nathan gripped the object that had cost them so much: Connors' phone. The cracked screen reflected the dim light, and the faint scuff marks along its edges told the story of its violent retrieval. It felt heavier than it should have, like it carried the weight of everything they'd lost tonight.

He clenched his jaw as he turned the phone over in his hand, staring at it as though it might yield some answer—some justification for the horrors they had witnessed. But all it offered was silence, and in that silence, he could still hear Ellie's screams.

"Nathan! Jennie! Please! Help me!"

Her voice was raw and desperate, echoing endlessly in his mind. He could still see the terror in her eyes, the blood streaking her face, and the way her outstretched hands had reached for him as the shadows closed in.

Across from him, Jennie sat strapped into her seat, her back pressed stiffly against the cabin wall. She watched him carefully, her gaze tracing the hard lines of his face. The Nathan she knew was always in control, always the pillar of strength their team relied on. But tonight, she saw cracks in the armor.

“Nathan,” Jennie said softly, her voice barely audible over the roar of the rotors. He didn’t respond. His eyes stayed fixed on the phone in his hand, his thumb brushing absentmindedly over the jagged crack on its screen.

“Nathan,” she repeated, firmer this time. Her tone cut through the haze, and his head jerked up slightly. He met her gaze, and she saw it: the guilt, the anger, the helplessness he was trying so hard to suppress.

“You still hear her, don’t you?” she asked, tilting her head slightly.

Nathan didn’t answer immediately. His shoulders sank as he exhaled sharply, the air fogging faintly in the frigid cabin. “Yeah,” he admitted finally, his voice rough. “I hear her. I see her. Every damn second.”

Jennie leaned forward, her harness pulling taut as she closed the space between them. Her breath came out in faint plumes as she spoke, the cold biting at the edges of her words. “You got the phone,” she said firmly. “You did what you came here to do.”

He shook his head, a bitter laugh escaping his lips. “What good is this phone, Jennie? It doesn’t bring her back. It doesn’t fix what happened.”

Jennie’s eyes softened, though her tone remained steady. “It’s not about fixing it, Nathan. It’s about making sure it doesn’t happen again. That phone—it has the proof we need. The creature, the attack, everything. Because of you, we have something to fight with.”

Nathan let out a slow breath, his grip on the phone tightening. "If we'd gotten there sooner—"

Jennie cut him off, her voice rising slightly. "Stop. Don't do this to yourself." She leaned in closer, her face lit faintly by the red glow. "You've been doing this long enough to know you can't save everyone. But how many lives have you saved, Nathan? How many people are still breathing because you were there?"

"It's not enough," he said quietly, his voice barely above a whisper.

"It's never enough," Jennie replied, her voice softening. "But we keep going. We have to."

The helicopter jolted slightly as they hit a patch of turbulence, shaking them in their seats. Nathan steadied himself, the cold steel of the cabin pressing against his back. The tension between them hung heavy in the air, a weight neither of them could ignore.

Jennie's voice broke the silence again, quieter this time. "Nathan, you and I started this together. You've carried me through hell more times than I can count. Let me carry some of this for you."

Nathan looked at her, really looked at her, and saw the raw sincerity in her eyes. They'd been through so much together—drafted into Phantom at the same time, surviving the grueling training, and fighting side by side through countless nightmares. She was more than a teammate; she was his anchor.

The faint crackle of the comms interrupted their moment, and the pilot's voice cut through. "We're ten minutes out from base."

Jennie leaned back into her seat, her gaze lingering on Nathan. He nodded faintly, but his grip on the phone didn't loosen. Outside, the base's lights shimmered faintly on the horizon, a beacon of safety in the endless dark. But Nathan's mind was still in the forest, with Ellie's screams echoing through the trees.

Revenge - Part 2

Outside, the base’s lights shimmered faintly on the horizon, a beacon of safety in the endless dark. But Nathan’s mind was still in the forest, with Ellie’s screams echoing through the trees. The crackle of the comm broke the heavy stillness, and Central's operator spoke, their voice steady but carrying an edge of caution.

"Commander Nathan, this is Central Command. We need to discuss a critical update."

Nathan straightened, his jaw tightening. “Go ahead.”

The voice on the other end hesitated briefly before continuing. “First, let me extend our deepest condolences for what happened to Ellie. She was—”

“Don’t,” Nathan cut in, his voice sharp. “Just tell me the update.”

Jennie’s gaze shifted between Nathan and the comm panel. She gripped the strap of her harness tightly, her gut already telling her this wasn’t good.

There was a pause, the line filled only with static for a moment too long.

“The tracker you deployed on the target went offline approximately ten minutes after your departure,” the voice finally said.

Nathan's expression darkened, his tone simmering with irritation. "And you're just telling me this now? Why wasn't I informed immediately?"

"We assumed it was a temporary issue and didn't want to distract you during extraction," the operator explained, the nervousness in their voice poorly concealed.

Nathan exhaled sharply, his anger barely restrained. "Temporary? Ellie's dead, and one of my men is gone, and you thought sitting on this was a good idea? Unbelievable."

Jennie shifted uncomfortably but stayed quiet, her eyes fixed on Nathan's clenched fists. She had seen him angry before, but this was different. This was personal.

"Sir," the operator interrupted cautiously, "it's not just the tracker going offline. Five minutes later, it came back."

Nathan froze, his brow furrowing. "Where?" he demanded, his voice dropping into a cold, dangerous tone.

Another pause.

"Outside Sarah's hotel."

The words hit Nathan like a sledgehammer. His body stiffened, and Jennie's eyes widened in alarm. She leaned forward slightly, her hand instinctively going to his arm.

“You’re telling me it’s at Sarah’s hotel,” Nathan said, his voice now a low growl. “And you waited this long to report it? She’s our primary objective! How in the hell does it know where she is?!”

The operator’s voice faltered, trying to maintain professionalism under Nathan’s fury. “We don’t know, sir. But the signal is strong, and it hasn’t moved.”

“Oh no,” Jennie murmured, horror creeping into her voice. She looked at Nathan, her expression stricken. “It’s with Sarah, isn’t it?”

Nathan turned his steely gaze to Jennie, then back to the comm. “Central,” he barked, his voice cutting through the cabin like a whip, “get an SUV prepped at the pad. I’m taking Jennie and another operative directly to the site the moment we land. Double the hotel guard and send reinforcements now. That thing is officially in the Red Zone.”

“Understood,” the operator replied hurriedly. “We’re mobilizing now.”

Nathan slammed the comm off and leaned forward, his head dropping into his hands for a moment before he looked up at Jennie. His voice was low, almost a growl. “I want her alive. No matter what.”

Jennie nodded, her expression resolute. “We’ll get there in time, Nathan.”

The helicopter had barely touched down when Nathan unlatched his harness, the cabin door sliding open with a metallic groan. He leapt onto the tarmac, Jennie close behind, followed by their third operative —a tall, sharp-eyed soldier known for his quiet precision. Without a word, they piled into the waiting SUV, the engine already running, its headlights cutting through the night.

Nathan slammed the door shut and barked, "Central, patch the signal to Jennie's handheld now!"

The tires screeched as the SUV roared forward, cutting through the compound gates and out into the deserted roads leading toward the city. Jennie fumbled with her device as the GPS feed loaded, her hands steady despite the urgency crackling through the air.

"It's up," she said, her voice tight. "The signal's behind the hotel… it hasn't moved."

Nathan's knuckles whitened as he gripped the steering wheel, his jaw clenched. "What the hell is it doing?" he growled, his voice laced with frustration and fury. "What is it waiting for?"

Jennie glanced at him but didn't respond, her focus locked on the glowing screen. The GPS beacon pulsed steadily, marking the location like a predator lying in wait.

The SUV skidded into the hotel's rear lot, tires screaming against the asphalt. Nathan killed the engine and threw the door open before the vehicle had fully stopped. Jennie and the third man followed in unison, rifles slung over their shoulders as they moved with trained precision.

"Central, keep the area lit," Nathan snapped into his comm, his voice low but commanding. Overhead, floodlights began to hum to life, bathing the edges of the wooded area in harsh white beams. Hotel security personnel were already mobilizing, sweeping the lot with flashlights and radios crackling.

Nathan shouldered his rifle, his gaze cutting through the chaos as he gestured for Jennie to follow. She nodded, motioning for their third operative to flank right. Together, they moved toward the shadows beyond the floodlights, where the signal remained unwavering.

"Sixty meters," Jennie whispered, glancing at her handheld. "Just beyond those trees."

Nathan raised a clenched fist, signaling a halt. They crouched low, their boots whispering against the damp grass. The scent of iron hung faintly in the air, subtle but unmistakable. The floodlights couldn't reach this far, leaving the area veiled in near-total darkness.

"Eyes open," Nathan murmured, his voice a steady rumble. His gaze swept the shadows, every branch and leaf shifting ominously in the faint breeze.

They moved as one, silent and deliberate, rifles raised. The tension was palpable, each step measured against the suffocating stillness. Jennie's grip on her weapon tightened as they reached the point marked on her device.

The ground was eerily quiet.

Nathan dropped into a crouch, his rifle angled down as he shone his flashlight onto the earth. A dark smear of blood glistened in the beam, fresh and vibrant against the grass. Beside it lay the tracker, its casing scratched but still intact, the LED blinking faintly.

He picked it up, holding it up for Jennie to see. She approached cautiously, her brows furrowing.

"What the hell—" she started, but Nathan cut her off, his voice sharp with realization.

"It knew," he growled. "That bastard knew it had a tracker."

Jennie's breath caught, her eyes darting toward the treeline as the weight of his words sank in. "And it left it here," she said slowly, her voice barely above a whisper. "Right outside Sarah's hotel."

Revenge - Part 3

Nathan's expression darkened, his jaw tightening as he clenched the tracker in his fist. "This isn't random," he muttered, his voice filled with cold certainty. "This is calculated."

Jennie knelt beside him, her eyes scanning the bloodstained ground. "What do we do, Nathan?" she asked, her voice steady but filled with urgency.

Nathan rose slowly, his gaze locked on the shadows ahead, the tracker still in his hand. "We adapt," he said, his tone unyielding. "But first, we make damn sure it's not coming back." Nathan pressed a finger to his earpiece, his voice low and sharp. "Central, this is Command. We've recovered the tracker. The bastard removed it and left it sixty meters from Sarah's hotel. It's deliberate."

The line buzzed with static before a voice replied, tense and clipped. "Understood, Command. Orders?"

"I want micro-cameras deployed around the entire perimeter. Every angle covered—no dead zones," Nathan barked, his tone leaving no room for negotiation. "And deploy a HOWLER. If it crosses into Red Zone again, it's war. I want eyes on every shadow within a ten-mile radius."

"Acknowledged," the operator responded. "HOWLER is on standby. Launching in ninety seconds. Micro-cameras en route."

Nathan exhaled sharply, shifting his grip on the tracker. Beside him, Jennie was already unpacking small, palm-sized cameras from her kit. She worked quickly, her movements precise, placing them on tree trunks and nearby surfaces, angling them to create an overlapping grid of surveillance.

Above them, the faint hum of the HOWLER's engines grew louder, the drone's blinking lights cutting through the darkness as it ascended into the sky. Controlled remotely via satellite, it zipped toward the dense forest, its infrared scanners ready to map every hidden movement.

"HOWLER is active," the operator confirmed through Nathan's earpiece. "Tracking patterns are online. We'll notify immediately if there's movement."

Jennie stepped back from her last placement, brushing dirt off her gloves. "That's all of them," she said quietly, motioning to the now-hidden cameras. "The area's sealed tight."

Nathan nodded, his gaze fixed on the treeline where the creature had last been seen—or where it wanted them to think it had been seen. The blood trail and discarded tracker were too precise, too deliberate. His gut churned with the realization that they were being toyed with.

Jennie approached cautiously, her voice soft but firm. "And Sarah? Are you going to tell her?"

Nathan's jaw tightened, his eyes narrowing. "No. Not yet."

Jennie tilted her head, her concern evident. "Why not? She has a right to know."

"She wouldn't believe me," Nathan said bluntly, his tone edged with frustration. "Even if I laid it all out, she wouldn't understand. Not now. Not without context."

Jennie studied him for a moment, her lips pressing into a thin line. "She'll figure out something's wrong, Nathan. She's not stupid."

"I know," he admitted, his voice softening. "But she's safer staying in the dark for now. She needs to hear it from John, not me."

Jennie's brows furrowed. "And John? Are you going to tell him?"

Nathan let out a dry laugh, shaking his head. "He'll know the second he looks at me. He always does."

Jennie fell silent, nodding in understanding. Their shared history with John ran deep, and she knew Nathan was right. The older man would see through any attempt to downplay the situation.

Nathan glanced at her, his expression resolute. "We hold our position for now. If it makes a move, we're ready. If it shows its face, we take it down. And if it gets near Sarah, I'm getting her to John."

Jennie straightened, her stance instinctively falling into that of a soldier ready to act. "And me?"

"You take over command until I'm back," Nathan said firmly. "Keep the team tight. No one moves without orders."

She nodded again, her resolve mirroring his. "Understood."

As the HOWLER's infrared beam swept the forest, casting an eerie red glow over the treetops, Nathan adjusted his rifle strap, his gaze hard and unyielding. He wouldn't let it win—not this time. The creature might have the upper hand in cunning, but he'd make sure it paid for every move it made.

And he'd ensure Sarah stayed alive to see the truth unfold.

Echoes of the Unknown - Part 1

Sarah hadn't slept much that night. Her thoughts churned in an endless loop, and every time she closed her eyes, the same jarring revelation returned: Nathan had been dead for over ten years—or so the world believed. Her journalistic instincts wrestled with her rational mind. If he was truly dead, how could he stand before her, alive, breathing, and speaking as though nothing had changed?

The weight of exhaustion clung to her as the early morning light filtered through the curtains. A low, rhythmic hum pierced the quiet—a sound that took her a moment to place. Helicopters. She pulled herself out of bed, her movements sluggish, and padded over to the window. Peeling the curtains aside, she froze.

It was a scene straight out of a military operation. Black armored vehicles were stationed around the hotel, their sleek surfaces glinting faintly in the dim light. Soldiers, clad in dark tactical gear, moved with practiced precision, their synchronized steps and alert gazes exuding an air of quiet authority. She spotted dog handlers patrolling the perimeter, the occasional glint of light catching on camera lenses being installed in strategic locations.

Her breath caught in her throat. She released the curtain and stepped back, her hands trembling at her sides. What the hell is going on?

A knock at the door snapped her from her spiraling thoughts. It was firm but measured, its cadence unsettlingly calm. She startled, her heart hammering against her ribcage. Drawing a shaky breath, she forced herself to approach the door and opened it.

Nathan stood on the other side.

He looked much the same as he had the last few days, but there was an undeniable change. Dark shadows ringed his eyes, betraying his lack of rest, and his normally confident posture seemed weighed down, burdened by something unspoken. And yet, there was still an air of command about him, a presence that demanded attention.

"Good morning," he said, his voice low and steady. He studied her for a moment, as if gauging her emotional state, before continuing, "I know it's a lot to take in. You need to eat something. After breakfast, we're heading to see John at the care facility."

Sarah opened her mouth to respond, but the words caught in her throat. The sound of the helicopters, the faint voices of soldiers outside—it all pressed in on her. Her gaze flicked back to Nathan's face, and unease crept up her spine. What are you not telling me? she wondered, the question lingering between them, unspoken but heavy.

Sarah hesitated before speaking, her gaze flicking between the bustling activity outside and Nathan's calm yet enigmatic demeanor. "What's going on out there?" she finally asked, her voice tinged with frustration. "Why all this military commotion?"

Nathan, ever the silent enigma, gestured for her to grab her coat. "We can talk over breakfast," he said simply. His quiet authority left little room for argument, and Sarah, grumbling internally, complied.

As they stepped out into the corridor, the air was cool and carried a faint smell of disinfectant mingled with the aroma of freshly brewed coffee wafting from the lower floors. Nathan walked ahead, his boots making dull, deliberate thuds against the polished wooden floor.

"I take it silence is your usual MO?" Sarah quipped, breaking the uneasy quiet as they approached the elevator.

Nathan glanced at her but said nothing, pressing the button for the ground floor. Sarah rolled her eyes and folded her arms, her frustration mounting.

When the elevator doors opened, the hum of activity in the lobby hit her immediately. Soldiers in black tactical gear moved with precision, their movements almost choreographed. Their radios crackled with clipped commands, and the occasional bark from a working dog echoed across the cavernous space. Sarah's stomach twisted uneasily as she followed Nathan.

"You're not going to tell me what all this is about, are you?" she asked, quickening her pace to match his long strides.

Nathan slowed and turned slightly, his expression unreadable. "Breakfast first," he said, his tone leaving no room for negotiation.

They walked through a side hall that opened into a dining area. The restaurant was eerily quiet compared to the chaos outside. Pristine white tablecloths gleamed under the soft glow of chandeliers, and the faint hum of jazz played in the background. A few staff moved with robotic efficiency, setting tables and preparing coffee stations.

Nathan led her to a table near the large windows, where she could still see the commotion outside. As they sat down, Sarah couldn't help but scan every detail. Soldiers stationed at strategic points, handlers walking dogs in precise circuits, and vehicles idling with their engines softly rumbling.

When Nathan returned with two cups of coffee and a small plate of food for her, she took a moment to gather her thoughts before diving in.

"Is all this really necessary?" she asked, her tone dripping with sarcasm as she gestured toward the window.

Nathan blinked, his calm composure betraying a flicker of confusion. "What?" he asked.

"This," Sarah said, setting her coffee down with a deliberate clink. She gestured toward the scene outside, then at the luxurious surroundings of the restaurant. "The hotel, the suite, the staff who seem programmed to cater to your every whim. Don't tell me you think I haven't noticed."

Nathan's lips twitched, almost forming a smirk. For a moment, she thought he might actually laugh, but instead, he leaned back in his chair, his silence speaking louder than any words could.

Sarah leaned forward, narrowing her eyes. "Typical," she muttered, picking up her coffee again, but not before sneaking another glance outside.

Echoes of the Unknown - Part 2

Sarah's voice sharpened, cutting through the calm of the luxurious dining room. "Come on, Nathan! I know your background. But why? Why all this secrecy?"

Nathan's calm, stoic expression faltered for just a fraction of a second before his gaze dropped to the table. "What do you think you know about me?" he asked quietly, his tone low and deliberate.

Sarah let out a frustrated sigh, her fingers tapping restlessly against the edge of her coffee cup. Her voice softened, but her determination remained unyielding. "You've been declared dead for almost ten years, Nathan. Your family buried you, grieved for you. And now, here you are, alive, sitting across from me as if none of it happened. Why?"

Nathan's jaw tightened, his knuckles whitening as he gripped the table's edge. He scanned the room quickly, as if ensuring no one could overhear. But there was no hiding the interest of nearby staff—two servers paused mid-step, their eyes flicking nervously between the two of them as though witnessing an argument they shouldn't. Nathan shot them a glance, and they quickly averted their eyes, moving away with hurried precision.

He leaned back slightly, his broad shoulders visibly tense. "It's not as simple as you think, Sarah," he said at last, his tone carefully measured. "Everything has its reasons—reasons that require drastic actions. Sometimes, sacrifices have to be made. Sometimes... those sacrifices hurt the people we care about."

“Sacrifices?” Sarah’s voice rose slightly, drawing the attention of a passing staff member, who hesitated before retreating discreetly. “Is that what you call what you did to your family? What you’ve been doing to me?”

Nathan’s calm mask cracked, and his brow furrowed. He seemed to weigh his words carefully. “You don’t understand—”

“Then make me understand!” Sarah interrupted, leaning closer across the table. “Stop dodging my questions, Nathan! Who are you? Or maybe a better question is—who are you people?”

Nathan froze. For the first time since they’d met, he looked truly rattled. His jaw worked as if chewing on words he didn’t want to say. His hand gripped his coffee cup so tightly she thought it might shatter.

“You think I haven’t noticed the emblems on their uniforms? The way everyone here hangs on your every word like it’s gospel?” Sarah continued, her tone relentless. “You’ve got more power, more resources than anyone I’ve ever met. Soldiers, vehicles, technology I’ve only seen in movies. And yet, here you are, pretending you’re just another cog in the machine. So don’t insult my intelligence, Nathan. Who are you?”

Nathan glanced out the window, his face a mask of restrained frustration. Outside, the faint hum of activity continued as soldiers patrolled the grounds, their movements precise and deliberate. One handler paused, his trained canine sniffing the air and letting out a low growl. The handler’s sharp command brought it to heel, but the scene only heightened Sarah’s unease.

"I can't tell you everything, Sarah," Nathan said finally, his voice almost a whisper. He didn't meet her eyes, instead staring at the faint swirl of steam rising from his coffee. "Not because I don't want to, but because there are things—things that even knowing would put you in more danger than you already are."

"That's bullshit, Nathan, and you know it!" Sarah's voice cracked, a mix of anger and desperation. She gestured wildly toward the window. "You think this—" she motioned to the soldiers, the vehicles, the surveillance equipment "—isn't already dangerous? You think I don't see what's happening here? I'm a target, and you know why. The least you can do is tell me the truth!"

Nathan finally looked at her, his eyes sharp and piercing, yet tired in a way that hinted at the weight he carried. "And what would you do with the truth, Sarah?" he asked, his voice steady but low. "Would it make you feel safer? Because it won't. It will only make you feel more helpless."

Sarah's breath hitched at the intensity in his gaze, but she refused to back down. "I'll take helpless over being lied to, Nathan. At least then I'd know what I'm up against."

Nathan leaned forward, his voice dropping to a near growl. "You think I haven't tried to protect people before? That I don't know what it's like to lose everything because someone knew too much?"

The tension between them was palpable, thick as the silence that followed his words. Sarah stared at him, her anger still simmering, but she could see something else in his expression now—pain, regret, and something that almost looked like fear.

"I've seen enough death to last a lifetime," Nathan continued, his voice softer now, almost breaking. "I've made choices you can't begin to imagine. And yes, they've cost me more than I care to admit. But if keeping you in the dark keeps you alive, then so be it."

Sarah exhaled shakily, leaning back in her chair. Her gaze flicked to the window again, watching as the soldiers continued their meticulous movements. "And what happens when I find out on my own?" she asked quietly.

Nathan didn't respond immediately. Instead, he sat back, his hands resting on the table as he studied her. The weight of his silence felt heavier than any argument they could have had.

"Then I hope you're ready for the consequences," he said finally.

A quiet but firm knock at the door broke the moment. Both of them turned as a young woman with her hair neatly tied back stepped into view. She glanced between Nathan and Sarah, her expression neutral but her posture confident.

"Excuse me," she said, her tone polite but authoritative. "You must be Sarah. My name's Jennie, and your transport is ready."

Sarah blinked, startled by the sudden presence of someone who had approached so silently she hadn't noticed. Struggling to regain her composure, she stammered out, "Oh... uh... hi."

Jennie offered a small, polite smile. "I'll be driving you and Nathan to your destination."

Nathan stood abruptly, draining the last of his coffee in a quick gulp before setting the cup back on the table with precision. He nodded to Jennie. "Thank you."

She acknowledged him with a slight nod in return, her movements as efficient and calculated as her words. Sarah, still processing the intrusion, pushed back her chair and stood. Her irritation boiled beneath the surface—she hadn't finished her conversation with Nathan, and now this mysterious newcomer was whisking them away.

Without a word, Sarah strode toward the door, her annoyance evident in the clipped rhythm of her steps. Nathan fell in beside Jennie as they followed her, his tone low but clear. "Good timing," he said.

Jennie's response was a simple nod, her expression unreadable as always. Outside, the activity was relentless. Soldiers moved in coordinated patterns across the grounds, their dark uniforms blending seamlessly with the black SUVs and tactical equipment. A handler walked briskly with a German Shepherd, the dog's ears twitching as it scanned the area. The air buzzed with a sense of controlled urgency, every movement purposeful, every detail scrutinized.

A sleek, black SUV was parked directly in front of the building's entrance. Jennie moved ahead, opening the back door for Sarah with a fluid motion. Sarah hesitated for a moment, her eyes darting between Nathan and Jennie. She climbed into the back seat, her gaze lingering on the organized chaos outside.

Jennie slid into the driver's seat with practiced ease, while Nathan took his place in the passenger seat. The door shut with a quiet thud, sealing them inside the vehicle's dim interior. For a moment, there was only the faint hum of the engine and the rhythmic click of Jennie fastening her seatbelt.

Echoes of the Unknown - Part 3

Sarah, sitting in the back, remained silent, her eyes flitting between Nathan and Jennie as the SUV rolled smoothly out of the compound. Her mind raced with unanswered questions, frustration bubbling beneath the surface. Who was this woman? How was she connected to Nathan? And more importantly, why was she part of whatever this operation was?

Nathan glanced back at Sarah briefly, but her expression remained unreadable. Beside him, Jennie navigated the vehicle with quiet focus, her hands steady on the wheel. The weight of unspoken words hung heavy in the air as the SUV sped down the secure road, leaving the fortified hotel behind.

Sarah finally broke the silence, her voice laced with suspicion. "So, is this how it's always going to be, Nathan? Me being left out of everything while you and your… team make all the decisions?"

Nathan didn't answer immediately. Instead, he looked out the window, the faint reflection of his face betraying no emotion. "You're not out of anything, Sarah," he said quietly. "You're in the middle of it, whether you like it or not."

Jennie's eyes flicked briefly to Nathan, then back to the road. She said nothing, but the faintest hint of a smirk tugged at the corner of her lips, as if she found some humor in Sarah's defiance.

Sarah leaned back against the seat, crossing her arms. "I'm starting to think I should've asked more questions before agreeing to come here."

Nathan's lips twitched into the ghost of a smile. "You'd still have ended up in the same place."

Sarah huffed, looking out the window as the landscape blurred past. She wasn't sure which was more frustrating—the cryptic answers, the growing sense of danger, or the fact that, despite everything, she felt a strange pull toward trusting Nathan.

The tension in the vehicle was palpable, but none of them spoke again as they drove on toward whatever awaited them at their destination. The SUV cruised onto the main road, the city quickly giving way to dense forest as they headed toward the outskirts. Sarah cleared her throat, breaking the silence. "So, Jennie," she began, her voice deliberately casual, "do you always sneak up on people, or was that just a special treat for me this morning?"

Jennie didn't look back, her eyes fixed on the road ahead. "I wasn't sneaking," she said simply, her tone as flat as her expression.

"Oh, really?" Sarah shot back, leaning forward slightly. "Because from where I'm sitting, you've got the stealth thing down to an art."

Nathan shifted slightly in his seat, but he didn't interject. His gaze remained forward, his jaw tight as if bracing himself for the conversation. Sarah turned her attention to him, her frustration growing. "And you," she said pointedly, "you just let her swoop in like that? I thought we had an understanding."

Nathan's lips twitched, but he said nothing.

"Of course," Sarah muttered, leaning back against the seat. She crossed her arms, glaring out the window at the passing scenery. The forest grew denser as they drove, the trees towering above them, their branches intertwined to create a canopy that blocked out most of the sunlight.

The car hit a small bump, and Sarah's eyes flicked to the dashboard. The radio, which had been playing faint static, crackled to life, the voice of a weather reporter cutting through the noise. "...scattered storms expected later this evening, with strong winds moving through the region…"

Jennie reached out and adjusted the volume, muting the voice. The sudden quiet made the tension in the car feel even heavier. Sarah exhaled sharply, running a hand through her hair. "You know," she said, her tone tinged with sarcasm, "this whole silent routine you two have going on? Super comforting."

Jennie's eyes met hers briefly in the rearview mirror. "We're focused," she replied, her words clipped.

"Focused on what?" Sarah pressed. "On not telling me anything?"

Nathan finally turned his head slightly, his gaze meeting Sarah's. "You'll understand soon enough," he said, his voice low and deliberate.

Sarah let out a dry laugh. "Right. Because that's not cryptic at all."

The road narrowed as they entered the forested outskirts. The towering trees seemed to close in around them, their shadows stretching across the road like grasping fingers. Sarah couldn't help but feel a chill despite the warmth of the morning sun.

Ahead, the care facility's gates came into view. The high, reinforced fence loomed like a sentinel, its sharp edges gleaming faintly in the light. Sarah watched as Jennie tapped a nearly invisible earpiece, her voice calm as she announced their arrival. "We're here."

The steel gates groaned as they began to slide open, the grinding sound of heavy machinery echoing through the quiet forest. Sarah leaned closer to the window, her eyes narrowing as she took in the scene. Armed guards patrolled the perimeter, their movements precise and deliberate. Security cameras tracked every angle, their lenses gleaming like watchful eyes.

"What kind of care home needs this level of security?" Sarah muttered, more to herself than anyone else. She caught Nathan glancing at her from the corner of his eye, but he didn't say anything.

The SUV rolled through the gates and into the compound. The gravel crunched under the tires as they came to a stop in front of the main building. Sarah's hand was already on the door handle, ready to escape the stifling confines of the car, but Jennie beat her to it. In one swift motion, Jennie exited the vehicle and opened Sarah's door.

Sarah hesitated, her frustration bubbling to the surface. "I can open my own door, thanks," she said sharply as she stepped out.

Jennie didn't respond, her face impassive as she moved to the back of the SUV, retrieving a sleek black case. Sarah turned her attention to Nathan, who had just stepped out of the passenger side. He stood for a moment, his eyes scanning the compound, taking in every detail as though committing it to memory.

Before Sarah could say anything, Jennie approached Nathan, holding out a slim black phone. Sarah froze, watching the exchange with growing suspicion.

"In case," Jennie said softly, her voice low enough that Sarah almost didn't catch the words.

Nathan's brow furrowed. "In case of what?"

Jennie's expression darkened. "After last night, nothing's certain anymore."

Nathan sighed, slipping the phone into his pocket. "Let's hope it doesn't come to that."

Sarah's chest tightened as she watched their interaction. The familiarity between them was palpable, and it left her with more questions than answers. What weren't they telling her? And why did she feel like she was being kept in the dark about something far bigger than she'd imagined?

The distant rumble of engines drew all their attention. Sarah turned to see a convoy of military vehicles approaching the compound. Soldiers disembarked with practiced efficiency, taking up positions around the area. Their presence was stark and unsettling, even compared to the already formidable security measures.

Nathan's jaw tightened as he turned to Jennie. "These aren't ours."

Jennie shook her head. "No. They're not."

"Then what are they doing here?" Nathan demanded, his voice low but edged with frustration.

Jennie's eyes tracked the soldiers as they moved. "I don't know. But if they're not careful, they'll bring more trouble than they're prepared for."

Sarah, still standing by the car, called out to Nathan. "Are you coming, or are you going to keep whispering state secrets?"

Nathan glanced back at Jennie, who gave him a subtle nod. He turned to follow Sarah toward the building, his steps deliberate and heavy.

As they entered the care facility, Sarah's mind raced. The strange tension, the cryptic exchanges, the uninvited military presence—everything felt like a puzzle with missing pieces. And she was determined to find out exactly what those pieces were.

Echoes of the Unknown - Part 4

As they stepped into the dimly lit corridor of the care facility, the heavy door closed behind them with a metallic thud. Sarah's eyes darted toward the thick walls and reinforced windows, her thoughts racing. She turned abruptly to Nathan, her voice sharp.

"Are those soldiers with you?" she demanded, gesturing toward the gate where the military vehicles had stopped.

Nathan, his expression as unreadable as ever, glanced briefly in the direction of the noise outside. "No," he said flatly, shaking his head. "I know who they are, but I have no idea why they're here."

Sarah's frustration bubbled to the surface. "That's not exactly reassuring," she said, her tone laced with sarcasm. "Why does this place even need a military presence?"

Nathan opened his mouth to respond, but the sound of footsteps approaching drew their attention. John emerged from a doorway further down the hall, his face a mix of curiosity and concern. The soft overhead lighting cast shadows across his lined features, making him appear older than Sarah remembered from their previous meetings.

"What's going on out there?" John asked, his gaze shifting between Sarah and Nathan. His voice carried the weariness of a man who had seen far too much.

Sarah looked to Nathan, expecting him to take the lead, but his silence spoke volumes. John sighed heavily and gestured toward the room behind him. “Sarah, why don’t you head inside for now? I’ll be in shortly.”

Sarah hesitated, her instincts screaming at her to stay and demand answers, but something in John’s tone made her pause. Reluctantly, she nodded and stepped past him into the room, casting one last glance at Nathan before disappearing inside.

The door clicked shut, leaving Nathan and John alone in the quiet hallway. John crossed his arms, his sharp eyes locking onto Nathan’s.

“What are they doing here?” he asked, his voice low but firm.

Nathan exhaled through his nose, his shoulders sagging slightly. “I don’t know,” he admitted, shaking his head again. “Something must’ve made them think this place is at risk. I wasn’t told anything about their deployment.”

John’s frown deepened. “Risk of what, exactly? You don’t need me to remind you—this place is supposed to be secure. If they’re here, it’s because someone thinks otherwise.”

Nathan met John’s gaze, his lips pressing into a thin line. “I agree,” he said quietly. “But I don’t think they realize what kind of danger they’re inviting by showing up unannounced.”

John studied Nathan’s face for a long moment, his expression softening slightly. “And what about you? What’s going on, Nathan? You look like you’ve been through hell.”

Nathan's jaw tightened, and for a moment, he looked as though he might brush off the question. But something in John's steady gaze seemed to disarm him. He ran a hand over his face, the weight of the last twenty-four hours evident in his every movement. "It's a long story," he said finally.

"I've got time," John replied, leaning slightly against the wall. "You and I both know this isn't the kind of situation where we can afford to keep each other in the dark."

Nathan sighed, glancing toward the closed door where Sarah was waiting. He lowered his voice further, as though speaking the words aloud might make them more real.

"There were some kids," he began. "Teenagers. They broke into the reserve to party. They didn't know what they were walking into."

John's eyes narrowed. "And?"

Nathan hesitated before continuing. "Something found them. We were sent in to recover any evidence—and any survivors."

John's expression darkened. "Survivors?" he echoed, the word heavy with disbelief.

"We found one," Nathan admitted, his voice tinged with regret. "A girl. Barely old enough to understand what she'd seen."

John's breath hitched, and for a moment, he seemed lost in thought.

“That doesn’t make sense,” he said finally. “That thing doesn’t leave survivors.”

Nathan nodded grimly. “That’s what we thought, too. But she was there. Alive. Broken, but alive.”

“And?” John pressed, his tone demanding.

Nathan’s gaze dropped to the floor, his voice barely above a whisper. “We couldn’t save her.”

The words hung in the air like a physical weight. John’s hand clenched into a fist at his side, but his voice remained steady. “What happened?”

“She had information,” Nathan said. “Something she’d seen, something she was trying to tell us. But it didn’t matter. It came for her before we could get her out. We lost her, and one of ours.”

John closed his eyes, his face etched with pain. “Goddammit, Nathan.”

“I set a tracker on it,” Nathan continued, his tone resolute despite the guilt in his eyes. “It should’ve led us right to it. But then the signal went dark.”

John’s eyes snapped open. “Dark? How?”

Nathan shook his head. “That’s the thing—it didn’t stay dark. It came back. Strong. And guess where it showed up?”

John's expression shifted from confusion to horror. "No," he breathed. "Not..."

Nathan's silence was all the confirmation he needed.

"Jesus Christ," John muttered, running a hand through his graying hair. "That thing is smarter than we thought."

Nathan nodded. "Much smarter. It's been adapting, learning. And now..." He glanced toward the door again, his voice trailing off.

John followed his gaze. "Does she know?" he asked quietly.

Nathan shook his head. "Not yet."

John's eyes hardened. "And what happens when she does? You think she's ready for this, Nathan? You think she's ready to be dragged into the kind of hell we've been living in?"

Nathan met his gaze, his expression unreadable. "She has to be," he said simply. "We don't have a choice."

John studied him for a long moment before finally nodding. "I hope you're right," he said softly. Then, without another word, he pushed off the wall and stepped into the room, leaving Nathan alone in the hallway.

Hunted by Shadows - Part 1

John lingered in the doorway, his eyes following Nathan as he crossed the room and settled into a solitary chair in the far corner. Nathan's posture was as rigid as ever, his gaze steady but distant, fixed firmly on Sarah. John sighed deeply, shaking his head as if trying to dispel the unease that hung heavy in the air. After a moment, he stepped into the room and approached Sarah, who sat at a small table, her expression a storm of irritation and confusion. He lowered himself into the chair beside her with a heavy sigh, the wood creaking under his weight.

"I can see how this must be maddening for you," John began, his voice soft but tinged with sympathy. "Everything going on around you —cryptic conversations, secrets you're not privy to—I imagine it feels like the walls are closing in."

Sarah looked up from the coffee cup she'd been staring into, her sharp gaze locking onto his. "Maddening doesn't even begin to describe it," she replied, her voice laced with frustration. "All this cloak-and-dagger nonsense, people keeping me in the dark—it's not what I signed up for when I came here."

John nodded, leaning back slightly in his chair. "I understand," he said. "But believe me, Sarah, every bit of this has a reason. And I promise, in time, you'll get the answers you're looking for. The real question is, once you have them, what will you do with them?"

Sarah narrowed her eyes, her fingers tightening around the mug in front of her. "What's that supposed to mean?" she asked, her tone wary.

John held her gaze, his expression steady but tinged with sadness. "Knowing the truth—it's not always as liberating as people think," he said quietly. "Sometimes, it's a burden. And once you know it, you can't un-know it. That's why Nathan has been... careful. Why he's drawn those lines around you."

Sarah let out a bitter laugh, shaking her head. "Careful? Lines? That's putting it lightly," she shot back. "It feels more like he's built a prison around me."

John gave a small smile, though it didn't reach his eyes. "You're not a prisoner, Sarah. You're free to leave anytime you want. But as long as you're here, seeking answers, we need to make sure you stay safe. You might not see it yet, but you're at the center of something dangerous."

Sarah leaned back in her chair, her eyes darting toward Nathan in the corner. His stoic figure looked carved from stone, unyielding and unapproachable. Her frustration bubbled to the surface, and she turned back to John. "Safe from what?" she demanded. "Why not just tell me the truth outright? I'm not some fragile thing that needs to be protected."

John's expression darkened slightly, his gaze dropping to the table. He paused for a moment before speaking, his voice low. "Sarah, you have no idea what you're up against. There are forces at play here—forces that don't care about the rules, about decency, or about the lives they destroy. If we could protect you by keeping you in the dark a little longer, we'd do it in a heartbeat."

The room seemed to grow colder, the air heavier. Sarah took a deep breath, trying to steady herself, but the tension was almost palpable. "I'm not asking to be coddled," she said firmly. "I just want to understand what's going on, who's after me, and why Nathan and his 'team' think I'm so important. Is that too much to ask?"

Nathan shifted slightly in his chair, the quiet creak breaking the stillness of the room like a shot. His expression didn't change, but the slight movement seemed to echo the weight of everything left unsaid.

John exhaled, standing and moving toward the window. His broad shoulders seemed to sag under an invisible weight as he gazed out into the bleak landscape beyond. "You'll get your answers," he said finally, his voice barely above a whisper. "But you need to be prepared for what they'll cost you. The truth... it doesn't come cheap."

Hunted by Shadows - Part 2

John leaned heavily against the window frame, his eyes scanning the barren landscape outside. The faint rays of the morning sun did little to warm the room, and the cold seemed to seep into his words as he spoke. "There are things out there, Sarah," he began, his tone low and weighted. "Things that you wish didn't exist. And if you knew the full extent of it, you'd wish you never had to learn."

Sarah drew a slow, deliberate breath, her frustration barely kept in check. "All I want," she said, her voice trembling slightly despite her best effort, "is to understand who's after me, who did this to you, and how you were the only one to come out of that place alive."

John turned slightly, his weathered face marked by lines of grief and experience. He glanced at Nathan, who gave him a nearly imperceptible nod, his expression unreadable. It was a silent acknowledgment, one that carried the weight of shared horrors.

"You already know how we ended up there," John began, his voice taking on a distant quality as though he were recounting a nightmare. "It was supposed to be a quiet trip, my family and I. We sat in the queue, surrounded by others waiting to get in—a ranger who never showed up, a couple planning to hike and camp, and a lone man parking his car before setting off on a long trek into the wilderness. Nothing seemed out of the ordinary at first."

He paused, his hand brushing against the windowpane, as though grounding himself in the present. "But the forest," he continued, his voice dropping to a near whisper, "it felt... wrong. Like something had been drained from it. The air was heavy, suffocating, and the silence wasn't peaceful. It was unnatural. The kind of quiet that makes the hair on your neck stand up."

Sarah shifted uncomfortably, the weight of his words pressing against her chest. "What do you mean?" she asked, her voice soft but insistent.

John turned to face her fully now, his gaze steady but haunted. "The woods were alive in the worst possible way," he said. "At night, it wasn't just the usual rustling of leaves or the occasional animal call. There was this... knocking. In the trees. Slow, deliberate, like a predator tapping its claws before striking. And then there was the feeling—the overwhelming, suffocating feeling that something was watching. Not just watching, but calculating."

"Calculating?" Sarah echoed, her voice faltering slightly.

John nodded, his expression grim. "Especially when I was with my kids. It was like I could feel its eyes, measuring every movement, every weakness. It wasn't random, Sarah. Whatever was out there—it was planning. Waiting for us to make a mistake."

The room fell silent for a moment, the only sound the faint creak of the building settling around them. Sarah crossed her arms tightly over her chest, trying to shake the goosebumps rising on her skin. She let out a nervous laugh, though it lacked any real humor. "You're talking like this is some kind of ghost story."

John's gaze didn't waver. "This isn't a story, Sarah," he said firmly.

"It's what's out there. It's real, and it's smart. Smarter than we ever imagined. Every move you make, it sees. It learns. And it doesn't stop until you've made a mistake it can exploit."

Sarah's hand tightened around her mug, her knuckles whitening. The room seemed colder now, though she couldn't tell if it was the chill in John's voice or the vividness of his words. "And those people?" she asked quietly. "The couple, the man, the ranger... what happened to them?"

John's shoulders sagged slightly, and he turned back to the window, his breath fogging the glass. "Each one has a story," he said softly. "Some never made it to their campsite. Others were found, or what was left of them, in places they should never have been. And the rest?" He hesitated, his voice catching slightly. "They just vanished."

Nathan, who had remained silent until now, shifted in his seat. His presence loomed over the conversation, a heavy reminder that there was more to the story than John was willing to share in that moment.

Sarah exhaled shakily, brushing her hair back from her face. "You're saying it's... hunting us?" she asked, her voice barely above a whisper.

John turned back to her, his face set in a grim mask of resolve. "It's not just hunting, Sarah. It's winning."

John's gaze lingered on Nathan, his expression conflicted. Nathan, sensing the hesitation, leaned forward slightly, his voice firm yet quiet. "Tell her," he said, his eyes locking with John's. "She deserves to know."

John sighed deeply, running a hand over his face as if trying to wipe away the weight of the memories. His shoulders sagged, and for a moment, he looked far older than his years. "I didn't want to drag you into this, Sarah," he began, his voice low and filled with regret. "But you've come this far, and you need to understand what we're dealing with."

Sarah sat frozen, her eyes darting between the two men. "Understand what? What aren't you telling me?" she demanded, her voice shaking despite the steadiness she tried to project.

John's hand gripped the edge of the table as he leaned forward, his gaze piercing. "I heard them that night, Sarah. The campers. The screams…" His voice broke slightly, but he pushed on, the words tumbling out as if they had been locked inside for too long. "It wasn't just fear. It was something primal. Something I'd never heard before. And then... silence. A silence so complete, it was deafening."

Sarah's throat tightened, and she struggled to find her voice. "What do you mean? What happened to them?"

Nathan's voice cut in, low and deliberate. "They were hunted, Sarah. Played with like prey. It wasn't just an attack—it was a game."

John nodded, his jaw tightening as he continued. "I didn't see it happen, but I know what it's capable of. And the recovery team..." He stopped, his voice catching again. "What they found was beyond anything I could have imagined. It left pieces—just enough to send a message."

Sarah's breath hitched, her heart pounding in her chest. "A message?"

Nathan leaned back in his chair, his arms crossed. "To anyone who thought they could stop it. To remind us that it's not just an animal. It's smarter. It's crueler. And it doesn't stop."

The room fell into a suffocating silence, the weight of their words pressing down on Sarah like a physical force. She looked at John, her voice barely above a whisper. "Why didn't you tell me this sooner?"

John's gaze softened, and he looked away, his hand trembling slightly. "Because once you know, you can't unsee it. You can't unknow the things it's done. I wanted to spare you that, Sarah. I didn't want you to carry this."

But Sarah wasn't ready to back down. She leaned forward, her eyes sharp. "You think keeping me in the dark protects me? I'm already in this, John. I need to know."

John sighed again, his shoulders slumping further. "Fine," he said quietly, his voice barely audible. "You want to know? Then I'll tell you what I do know."

Nathan glanced at John, giving a small nod of approval, and John began to recount the horrors of that night.

The Silent Watcher

The tent stood firmly on the soft earth, its canvas glowing faintly in the last rays of the setting sun. Ben and Lily sat nearby, soaking in the serenity of the wilderness. The sky above shifted from warm oranges and pinks into deeper purples as the sun dipped behind the towering mountains. The crisp air carried the scent of pine and damp earth, mingling with the gentle murmur of a nearby stream.

The forest felt alive. Birds trilled in the distance, crickets began their rhythmic hum, and the occasional rustle of leaves marked the passage of unseen creatures. Lily stretched out with a deep breath, a small smile spreading across her face. "I don’t think I’ve ever felt so far away from everything," she murmured. "It’s like the rest of the world doesn’t even exist out here."

Ben grinned, settling beside her. "That’s the whole point, isn’t it? No people, no noise. Just us, the wilderness, and nothing else."

Lily nodded, gazing toward the horizon where the last remnants of light lingered. "It’s beautiful," she said softly. "Almost… too perfect."

Ben chuckled, nudging her shoulder playfully. "You’re not going to get all paranoid on me, are you? This is why we came here—peace, quiet, and a little adventure."

Despite his lighthearted tone, something unspoken lingered in the air. Lily couldn’t shake the nagging feeling that this quiet was… different. It wasn’t the peaceful stillness she loved in nature; it felt heavy, deliberate, as though the forest itself was holding its breath.

"I know it sounds silly," she said after a pause, "but doesn't it feel too quiet?"

Ben raised an eyebrow, his grin faltering slightly. "What do you mean? I thought that's what you wanted—no city noise, no distractions."

Lily hugged her knees, her gaze drifting toward the darkening treeline. "It's hard to explain. It's the kind of quiet that makes you feel like you're being watched."

Ben laughed, though there was an edge to it. "Come on, Lily. Who would be out here? It's just us."

But even as he said the words, he couldn't fully believe them. Something about the stillness gnawed at him, a faint unease he wasn't ready to admit.

As the sun finally disappeared, leaving only the faint glow of twilight, Ben got up to add logs to the fire. The flames crackled and danced, casting long, shifting shadows across the clearing.

"Tomorrow should be good," he said, his voice louder than necessary. "That ridge we saw earlier—bet we'll get an incredible view from up there."

Lily nodded absently, pulling her jacket tighter as the temperature dipped. The fire's warmth barely cut through the chill creeping in around them. "Yeah," she murmured, though her thoughts remained elsewhere.

The firelight flickered against the tent, pushing back the shadows that seemed to press in from all sides. The crickets sang their rhythmic tune, filling the void left by their conversation. Then, abruptly, the melody stopped.

Ben froze mid-motion, his ears straining against the deafening silence. "Lily," he whispered. "Do you hear that?"

She sat up, her heart pounding. "Why… why did it get so quiet?"

"It's nothing," Ben said quickly, though his voice wavered. "It's just nature being weird." He tried to laugh it off, but his eyes darted toward the treeline, scanning the dark.

Lily hugged herself, her breath shallow. "It feels like someone's watching us," she said, her voice barely audible.

Ben forced a chuckle. "Come on. Who would be out here, spying on us in the middle of nowhere?"

The words did little to ease the tension. Both of them felt it now—a suffocating presence in the dark. The shadows beyond the firelight seemed deeper, heavier, like something unseen lurked just beyond the edges of their vision.

"We should get some sleep," Ben said, his voice tight. "Long hike tomorrow."

They crawled into their sleeping bags, though neither could shake the feeling that something was wrong. Lily lay stiff, every creak of the forest and flutter of wind setting her nerves on edge. Despite her exhaustion, she stayed awake long after Ben's breathing slowed, her eyes fixed on the faint glow of the fire through the tent's fabric.

Hours passed before both of them woke to a low, rumbling vibration beneath them. Ben sat up instantly, his heart racing. "What the hell was that?"

Lily's wide eyes darted around the tent. "Something's out there," she whispered. "I heard something moving."

The vibration came again, stronger this time, accompanied by the distant snapping of branches. Heavy, deliberate footsteps echoed through the still night. A faint, labored snorting reached their ears, like the breath of something massive.

Ben scrambled out of the tent, pulling Lily with him. The cold night air bit at their skin as they stood in the clearing, frozen in place. Suddenly, a deer burst through the underbrush, its eyes wide with terror as it nearly crashed into them before vanishing into the woods.

Ben let out a shaky laugh, his breath visible in the cold. "Just a deer," he muttered. "Scared the hell out of me."

Lily didn't move. Her gaze remained fixed on the darkness. "It looked terrified," she said quietly.

Before Ben could respond, the ground shook violently. Branches snapped and trees groaned as a herd of deer thundered into the clearing. Their hooves tore up the earth, sending dirt and sand spraying into the fire. The flames died instantly, plunging the campsite into pitch darkness.

Ben’s voice was barely a whisper. "What’s happening?"

They stood motionless, their breaths shallow and rapid. After a moment, the forest began to settle. The crickets resumed their hum, and the faint chirping of birds returned.

"See?" Ben said shakily. "As long as the birds are singing, there’s no predators nearby. We’re fine."

But Lily didn’t answer. Her eyes remained locked on the trees, her face pale and drawn. They crawled back into the tent, though neither could relax. The oppressive quiet returned, wrapping around them like a shroud.

Ben drifted into a fitful sleep, only to jolt awake hours later at the sound of the zipper moving. His eyes flew open, his body rigid. The zipper on the tent’s entrance slid slowly downward, the faint metallic rasp filling the still air.

"Lily," he hissed. "Wake up."

She stirred groggily, but before she could speak, the zipper stopped. Two massive, clawed hands slipped through the opening, their shadowed forms illuminated faintly by the moonlight. They seized

Lily’s legs, yanking her halfway out of the tent.

She screamed, thrashing wildly. "Ben! What’s happening?!"

Ben lunged, grabbing her arms and pulling with all his strength, but whatever was on the other end was far stronger. He heard the sickening snap of bone as it tore at her legs, blood spraying across the canvas.

Her screams echoed through the forest, raw and desperate, before fading into a gurgled cry as the creature dragged her away. The tent collapsed partially around Ben as he sat frozen in shock, his hands trembling and slick with her blood.

Then he saw them—two glowing eyes staring back at him through the darkness.

The clawed hands returned, tearing through the fabric as they reached for him. His scream pierced the night, but it was swallowed by the forest, leaving nothing but silence behind.

Shadows

John exhaled deeply, his eyes fixed on the table before him. His voice, low and steady, carried the weight of memories he had long tried to bury. "That night..." he started, pausing as if searching for the right words. "I heard something." Sarah, perched on the edge of her chair, leaned in slightly, her pen poised over the notebook. "What did you hear?" she asked softly, careful not to disrupt the fragile flow of his recollection.

John's gaze shifted, his eyes distant, as though staring into the very heart of the dark forest. "It sounded like a scream. A cry for help—raw, desperate. It was faint... like it was being carried by the wind. But... I couldn't tell where it was coming from."

His words hung in the air like a specter. He paused, running a hand over his face. "The woods... they swallowed it. The sound just vanished, pulled into the darkness, into the shadows. I... I wasn't sure if it was real."

Sarah's pen faltered. For a moment, she didn't write. Her gaze locked onto his, as if trying to uncover the truth hidden beneath his words.

"You didn't go looking for it?" she asked, her tone even, devoid of accusation but tinged with curiosity.

John shook his head slowly, his voice almost inaudible. "I didn't know what I was hearing. It could've been the wind. Could've been my mind playing tricks on me. Or..." His words trailed off, his jaw tightening.

The room fell into a heavy silence, broken only by the faint creak of the wooden floor beneath Sarah's shifting weight.

"But now," John said finally, his voice thick with regret, "I know it was real. Someone was out there... someone needed help. And I did nothing. The forest—" he looked up, his eyes haunted, "—the forest had already claimed them. Just like it claims everything."

Under the dim light of the small room, John sat at the table, his hands gripping a steaming mug of coffee. The faint tremor in his fingers betrayed the composure he tried to maintain. Across from him, Sarah leaned forward slightly, her brows furrowed as she studied him. Nathan sat further back, in the shadowy corner of the room, his figure half-obscured, arms crossed, watching silently like a coiled spring ready to snap.

“John,” Sarah began carefully, her tone a mixture of concern and challenge, “do you need a break?”

Nathan's gaze shifted from the floor to Sarah, his eyes narrowing. He uncrossed his arms, leaning forward just enough for his silhouette to catch more of the light.

“We don't have time for breaks,” he muttered, his voice carrying an edge of irritation. “Not now.”

John let out a sharp exhale, lifting the mug to his lips for a long, deliberate sip. He set it down with a dull thud and shook his head.

"Nathan's right," he said, his voice low but firm. "We don't have time."

Sarah straightened in her chair, but her eyes didn't leave John. She could see the weariness etched into his face, the weight of untold truths pulling at his every word.

"What are you so afraid of, John? We're safe here, aren't we? There's a perimeter, fences, and more armed men than I can count outside." Her voice rose slightly, as though trying to convince herself as much as him.

John's lips twisted into a bitter smile. "Safe?" He shook his head slowly, his tone dripping with irony. "You don't know what safe is, Sarah. Not out here."

Nathan shifted in his corner, the chair creaking faintly beneath him. His voice cut through the tension, calm but biting.

"She doesn't get it, John. None of them do. They think it's just some animal. Something that can be tracked and put down."

John nodded solemnly, his eyes locking with Sarah's. "That's what I thought too, once. Until I realized... it's worse. It's smarter than that."

Sarah opened her mouth to respond, but her words caught in her throat. Her mind raced, trying to piece together the fragments John was giving her.

"You mentioned a hiker," she said finally, her voice quieter now. "Someone who went out into the wilderness. What happened to him?"

John leaned back in his chair, his eyes darkening as if the memories themselves were a weight pressing down on him.

“His name was Logan Wright,” John began, his voice hollow. “He loved the forest. Said it was his escape from the world. He parked his car by the trailhead, told his friends he’d be back in three days.” He paused, his hand tightening around the mug. “They found his car in a ditch two days later. No sign of him. No tracks, no clothes, nothing.”

Sarah’s lips parted, but no words came out. John pressed on.

“The only thing they found…” His voice faltered for a moment before he continued. “...was his wallet. Lying in the mud. Like it had been dropped there on purpose.”

Nathan’s chair scraped against the floor as he shifted again, his gaze now fixed on John.

“Did they search for him?” Sarah asked hesitantly.

John let out a bitter laugh, low and cold. “Of course they did. They combed the area for days. Found nothing. Not a trace. The forest doesn’t give anything back once it takes it.”

Sarah swallowed hard, the room growing colder with every word.

“What do you think happened to him?” she asked, almost in a whisper.

John's eyes met hers, filled with a sorrow and certainty that made her stomach drop. "I think he didn't stand a chance," he said. "I think it got him before he even realized he wasn't alone."

The silence that followed was suffocating. Sarah looked down at the notepad she'd been absently scribbling on. Her breath hitched as she saw the jagged shapes her hand had drawn without her noticing.

She tore her gaze away, back to John, whose focus had shifted to the table's surface, lost in thought. Slowly, he stood, his shoulders sagging as though the weight of his words had been too much.

"I need to show you," John said quietly, his voice heavy with the weight of what he was about to say. Rising slowly from his seat, he began pacing, his steps measured as if testing the strength of the floor beneath him. His hand brushed the edge of the table, lingering for a moment before he moved toward the window, the shadows outside pressing against the glass like silent spectators.

Nathan watched him from his seat in the corner, his expression unreadable but his eyes sharp, tracking every movement. Sarah sat frozen, her pen hovering above her notepad, her breath caught somewhere between fear and anticipation.

"If you want to understand," John continued, his voice lower now, each word deliberate, "we have to go back. Back to the beginning. To his point of view."

He turned from the window and faced them again, his silhouette dark against the pale light filtering through the curtains. "That hiker wasn't the first… and he sure as hell wasn't the last."

Sarah shifted uncomfortably in her chair, her fingers tightening around the notepad as though it might anchor her. She glanced at Nathan, whose expression remained grim, offering her no comfort. The room felt smaller, the air dense with the weight of unspoken horrors.

John returned to his chair but didn't immediately sit. Instead, he leaned heavily on the backrest, his knuckles white against the wood. "This isn't just about the forest," he said, his tone thick with resignation. "It's about what's in it. What's waiting."

Nathan's voice broke the tension, low and deliberate. "You still don't get it, Sarah. None of us really do. But you will."

The silence that followed Nathan's words was suffocating. Sarah could feel the weight of their gazes on her, the intensity of the room pressing in like a physical force. She lowered her pen, the notepad forgotten in her lap.

"What are you not telling me?" she asked, her voice quiet but insistent.

John looked at her, his face pale under the dim light. "There are things out there," he said slowly, as though tasting the words for the first time. "Things that don't leave evidence. Things that don't leave survivors."

Nathan leaned forward, his chair creaking ominously. "Logan Wright," he said simply.

Sarah frowned. "The hiker you mentioned earlier?"

John nodded, his expression hardening. "Logan wasn't the first. But his story… it's different. It's the one that stuck with me. The one I can't shake."

Sarah's grip tightened on the edges of her notepad. "What happened to him?"

John let out a slow breath, his gaze dropping to the table as if the wood itself held the answers. "He was an experienced outdoorsman. A guy looking for solitude, for some kind of escape. I didn't know him, not personally, but I've seen his type before. They come out here thinking they're going to find something—peace, adventure, maybe even themselves."

He paused, his jaw tightening. "They never expect the forest to find them first."

Sarah shivered involuntarily, the air in the room growing colder. "You said they found his car?"

John nodded again. "In a ditch, just off one of the old trails. It had been there for at least a day, maybe two. No signs of a struggle. No blood. Just his wallet on the ground outside the driver's side door, like he'd dropped it on his way out."

Sarah opened her mouth to speak, but John's words came faster now, the memories spilling out as if a dam had broken.

"They sent search parties. Dogs. Hell, they even had a helicopter out here for a day or two. But nothing. No tracks. No clothes. Not even the scraps you'd expect from an animal attack."

Nathan leaned back in his chair, the shadows shifting around him. "It's not like any animal we've ever seen."

John's hand tightened on the edge of the table. "I heard about it weeks later. By then, it was just another story, another unsolved mystery to add to the pile. But I couldn't stop thinking about it. About how quiet the forest had been that week. About the way the air felt heavier, like it was waiting for something."

He looked up, meeting Sarah's gaze. "I know what's out there now. And I think it found Logan before anyone else could."

Sarah swallowed hard, her mind racing. Her notepad sat untouched on her lap, the pen she'd been holding forgotten between her fingers. "What do you mean by that?" she asked, her voice barely audible.

John hesitated, the weight of his words hanging in the air. "I mean… Logan never stood a chance. And neither did anyone else who followed him."

The room fell into silence again, the only sound the faint hum of the wind outside. Sarah glanced down at her notepad and froze. Her hand had been moving unconsciously, sketching shapes in the margins. Eyes. Teeth. Claws.

She tore her gaze away, back to John, who was still staring at the table as if it might offer him some kind of absolution.

"Where do we go from here?" she asked finally, her voice trembling.

John's answer came slowly, each word measured and deliberate. "We go back to the beginning. To Logan Wright. To the night the forest claimed him."

Logan - Part 1

The red Chevy Silverado rumbled steadily along the dirt road, its tires crunching over loose gravel as the dense forest enveloped Logan Wright on all sides. At fifty-three years old, Logan was no stranger to these trails—or so he thought. This trip was supposed to be one of three he'd planned, a final push to find some challenge, some spark that made him feel alive again.

As he glanced between the road and the folded map on the passenger seat, a small smile played on his lips. The map highlighted his destination: a renowned ridge known for its breathtaking views and challenging climbs. It was said to be a magnet for experienced hikers, a true test of resilience. The forest around him was nothing short of mesmerizing. Sunlight filtered through the towering pine trees, their needles swaying gently in the breeze. The light danced like diamonds across the forest floor, a spectacle that seemed to banish all worries.

"This," Logan murmured, gripping the steering wheel tighter, "was the right call."

The forest grew denser as he drove further. Shadows stretched across the ground as the sun dipped closer to the horizon, its warm glow painting the sky in hues of gold and amber. He wanted to reach the trailhead before nightfall, and as the parking lot came into view, relief washed over him. It was empty. Quiet. Perfect.

He stepped out of the truck, the cool mountain air hitting him immediately. Taking a deep breath, he scanned the area. A large, weathered mapboard stood near the trailhead, its surface dotted with marked paths and notes from previous hikers. He approached it, tracing the route he had planned with his finger. The ridge he sought would take him through dense forest and up a steep incline. Exactly the kind of adventure he craved.

Logan grabbed his gear from the truck, slinging his backpack over one shoulder. The first steps onto the trail felt like a release. The gravel path beneath his boots, the distant sound of birdsong, the gentle rustle of leaves—it was all so alive. The warmth of the sun mixed with the cool breeze, creating the perfect balance. For the first time in a long while, Logan felt at peace.

The gravel path gave way to a narrow dirt trail flanked by dense underbrush. The deeper Logan went, the more the sunlight faded, replaced by the soft, muted glow of twilight. Beams of light pierced through the canopy like stage lights, illuminating patches of moss-covered ground. He paused for a moment, taking it all in. It felt almost otherworldly, like stepping into a storybook.

As the shadows deepened, a flicker of unease crept in. Reaching into his pocket, Logan frowned. "Where the hell's my phone?" he muttered, patting down his jacket and pants. A curse slipped from his lips as he realized he must have left it in the truck. "Damn it," he whispered. "I'll be fine. I've done this a hundred times."

The trail grew darker as the last light of the sun disappeared behind the mountains. Logan switched on his headlamp, its beam slicing through the growing gloom. A faint mist clung to the ground, swirling around his boots as he walked. The forest was quieter now. Too quiet.

Logan froze. The birdsong had stopped. So had the crickets. All he could hear was the faint crunch of his own footsteps. His breath quickened as he scanned the trees, the beam of his headlamp darting across twisted roots and towering trunks. His stomach twisted uncomfortably. He never got nervous on these hikes. But tonight felt... different.

"Come on, Logan," he muttered, shaking his head. "Get a grip."

He pressed on, but the silence was deafening. Each step seemed to echo, the sound amplified in the unnatural stillness. Then, a new noise —a faint, rhythmic crunch—stopped him in his tracks. It wasn't his own footsteps. It was something else. Something heavier.

His head snapped toward the sound, his heart pounding. The beam of his headlamp revealed nothing but shadows. He swallowed hard, forcing himself to keep moving. "It's just an animal," he whispered, trying to calm his racing thoughts. "Probably a deer."

But the sound followed him, keeping its distance, deliberate and unrelenting. His hands began to tremble as he gripped the straps of his backpack. Every nerve in his body screamed at him to run, but he forced himself to walk, each step heavier than the last.

Then, the breathing started. Low, guttural, and disturbingly close. Logan whipped around, his headlamp casting frantic beams of light across the trees. A shadow moved—just at the edge of the light. It was fast, too fast to make out.

His breath came in shallow gasps as he turned back toward the trail. "Just keep walking," he told himself, his voice barely audible. "Don't panic."

Logan - Part 2

But he couldn't stop himself. The sound of heavy footsteps grew louder, closer. Panic surged through him as he broke into a run, his boots slipping on the uneven ground. Branches snagged at his clothes, tearing fabric and skin as he tore through the forest. His heart thundered in his chest, the rhythm deafening in the stillness.

The footsteps behind him matched his pace, each one landing with a force that sent vibrations rippling up through the soles of his boots. Logan chanced a glance over his shoulder, the light from his headlamp bouncing erratically through the trees. His heart seized in his chest.

Two glowing red eyes stared back at him from the darkness, unblinking and unwavering. They didn't move. They didn't flinch. They just watched.

And then, as suddenly as they appeared, they vanished.

Logan's breath came in shallow, ragged gasps, his chest burning as he whipped his head forward again, focusing on the trail ahead. The beam of his headlamp illuminated the faint outline of the gravel path. He was close. His legs pumped harder, his entire body screaming at him to keep moving.

The parking lot finally came into view. The outline of his truck stood like a sanctuary in the encroaching darkness. Relief crashed over him as he skidded to a halt beside the driver's side door, fumbling desperately for his keys. His trembling fingers struggled to find the right one.

Cursing under his breath, he threw a glance back at the shadowy forest.

The key slid into the lock with a satisfying click, and Logan yanked the door open. He threw himself inside, slamming the door shut and locking it in one frantic motion. For a brief moment, the interior of the truck felt like a haven, the thick metal doors separating him from whatever had been stalking him.

Leaning back against the seat, Logan's breaths came in ragged bursts. The headlamp still strapped to his forehead cast a dim glow across the dashboard, illuminating the folded map and his phone lying on the passenger seat. Grabbing the phone, he tapped at the screen with trembling hands.

No service.

The words felt like a slap. Logan let out a frustrated growl, tossing the phone onto the seat. His eyes darted to the ignition. With a twist of the key, the engine roared to life, the familiar sound filling the cab. The headlights flared, illuminating the gravel path ahead. Gravel crunched under the tires as he shifted into drive and pressed the gas pedal.

The truck lurched forward, but something felt wrong. The engine growled low, the sound heavier and more strained than usual. Logan frowned, glancing at the dashboard. Everything appeared normal. Pressing the gas harder, the truck picked up speed, but a strange resistance remained, as if something unseen was holding it back.

Adjusting the rearview mirror, Logan's blood turned to ice.

Two crimson eyes stared back at him from the rear window. They hovered just beyond the glass, unblinking and impossibly close. Logan's breath hitched as a faint fog began to spread across the window. It wasn't condensation—it was breath. Something was breathing on the glass.

His trembling hands tightened on the steering wheel, his knuckles turning white. "Jesus Christ," he whispered, the words barely audible.

The fog thickened as the creature's breath steamed against the window, obscuring the glowing eyes. Then came the sound—a low, wet drag, like something heavy sliding across the glass. Logan didn't dare turn his head. His eyes remained glued to the rearview mirror as a smear appeared on the fogged surface.

A tongue.

It dragged across the glass with deliberate slowness, its thick, slimy texture leaving a glistening trail in its wake. Logan's stomach churned, bile rising in his throat. His hand darted to the gear shift, slamming it into reverse. The truck jerked backward before he threw it into drive and stomped on the gas.

The tires spun for a moment before catching traction. The truck surged forward, bouncing over the uneven gravel road. Logan gritted his teeth, his focus locked on the path ahead. He couldn't bring himself to look back, couldn't risk seeing those eyes again.

But he didn't have to look. The truck suddenly rocked violently, a deafening thud reverberating through the cab as something slammed into the side. Logan screamed, his hands jerking the wheel in an attempt to steady the vehicle. The beam from his headlamp flickered wildly, casting distorted shadows across the dashboard.

Another impact sent the truck skidding, its tires screeching as it careened off the road. Logan's head slammed against the steering wheel, stars bursting across his vision. Pain shot through his skull as warm blood trickled down his temple.

The truck settled with a groan, its frame tilted precariously in a ditch. Logan blinked rapidly, his vision swimming. Wiping at the blood on his face with a shaky hand, he struggled to orient himself.

"What... the hell... was that?" he muttered, his voice trembling.

Reaching for his phone, now lying on the floor of the cab, Logan's heart sank. The screen was cracked, the faint glow barely visible. He pressed the buttons, but the device refused to respond. Frustration and fear collided as he hurled the phone onto the passenger seat.

Logan forced himself to look out the windows, his headlamp casting faint beams into the darkness. The fog pressed against the glass, impenetrable and suffocating. He strained his ears, listening for any sign of movement, but the silence was absolute.

He couldn't stay in the truck. That much was clear. His mind raced as he remembered the map. There was a campsite—two kilometers away. It was his only chance.

Fumbling with the headlamp on his forehead, Logan adjusted its angle before reaching for the crumpled map on the seat beside him. The beam of light trembled as he spread it out over the dashboard. His finger traced the route to the campsite, his mind working frantically. Two kilometers. Two kilometers to safety.

His heart pounded as he glanced at the rearview mirror again. Nothing. The glass was clear now, the crimson eyes gone as if they'd never been there. But the memory of them burned in his mind, a searing brand of fear he couldn't shake.

Inhaling deeply, Logan forced air into his lungs and reached for the door handle. The metallic creak of the hinges echoed through the oppressive silence as he pushed the door open. He flinched at the noise, glancing nervously toward the surrounding trees. The forest remained still, the mist curling lazily at the edge of the headlights.

"Keep it together," he muttered to himself, stepping out of the truck. His boots crunched against the gravel, the sound unbearably loud in the otherwise silent night. The cold air bit at his exposed skin, and the smell of damp earth filled his nostrils. He tightened his grip on the map and headlamp, his other hand brushing against his pocket instinctively. His wallet was gone, but in his panic, he didn't notice.

Closing the door as quietly as he could, Logan winced at the faint click of the latch. Casting one last glance at the truck, he turned toward the forest path. The headlamp illuminated the way, casting long shadows that seemed to shift and writhe at the edges of the beam.

The first steps were the hardest. Each movement felt like a gamble, as if the very act of walking might summon whatever had stalked him. But as he moved further from the truck, his resolve hardened. He had to keep going. There was no other option.

Logan - Part 3

The path was uneven, the gravel giving way to dirt and roots that snagged at Logan's boots. The headlamp's beam danced across the terrain, illuminating twisted tree trunks and patches of moss. Logan's breath came in shallow bursts, his chest tight with fear.

Then he heard it—a faint rustle behind him.

He froze, his heart hammering in his chest. Slowly, he turned, the headlamp's beam cutting through the mist. The truck was barely visible in the distance, its red taillights a faint glow. But beyond that, there was nothing. No eyes. No shadow. Just the suffocating silence of the forest.

"Just your imagination," he whispered, his voice barely audible. "Keep moving."

He turned back toward the path and quickened his pace. The mist thickened around him, swirling like ghostly fingers. The beam of his headlamp seemed weaker now, its light swallowed by the darkness. Logan's mind raced with thoughts he couldn't control. What if it's still following me? What if it's waiting?

The sound came again, louder this time—a heavy, deliberate thud, like something stepping onto the path behind him.

Logan's blood ran cold. He didn't dare look back. His legs moved on their own, breaking into a frantic run. The map crumpled in his hand as he pumped his arms, his boots pounding against the dirt.

The footsteps behind him grew louder, each one landing with a force that shook the ground. Logan's breath came in ragged gasps, his lungs burning as he pushed himself harder. The headlamp's beam flickered, the light sputtering as if it might give out at any moment.

He risked a glance over his shoulder, and his stomach dropped.

The crimson eyes were back, closer than before. They blinked slowly, almost lazily, as if savoring the hunt. Logan stumbled, his boots catching on a root. He hit the ground hard, the impact knocking the wind out of him.

Scrambling to his feet, he forced himself to keep running. The path blurred around him, his headlamp casting frantic, jagged beams of light. His mind screamed at him to move faster, but his body was reaching its limit.

The campsite. Just get to the campsite. The thought pulsed in his mind like a mantra, driving him forward even as his legs threatened to give out.

Then, the footsteps stopped.

Logan skidded to a halt, his chest heaving as he strained to hear. The silence was deafening. He spun in place, the headlamp's beam sweeping the forest, but the crimson eyes were gone.

He took a hesitant step forward, his breath hitching as the sound returned—this time from ahead of him. A low growl rumbled through the air, vibrating in his chest. Logan's grip tightened on the headlamp as he aimed it forward.

The creature stepped into the light.

It was massive, its form shrouded in shadow and mist. The crimson eyes burned like twin embers, their gaze locked onto him with a terrifying intensity. Its maw hung open, revealing rows of jagged teeth that dripped with saliva. Logan's legs buckled as the full weight of his fear crashed over him.

"No," he whispered, his voice barely audible. "No, this can't be real."

Logan turned to run, but the creature was faster. A blur of black and crimson slammed into him, knocking him flat onto the forest floor. The air was forced from his lungs in a sharp gasp as he clawed at the dirt, desperate to escape. Before he could get up, the creature's massive claws wrapped around his ankle and yanked him back.

"No! No, please!" Logan screamed, his voice breaking as he was dragged across the rough ground. Twigs and rocks scraped against his skin, tearing through his clothes. He struggled wildly, kicking at the iron grip on his leg, but it was useless. The creature's strength was inhuman.

It stopped suddenly, flinging him into a small clearing. Logan landed with a sickening thud, pain shooting through his ribs. He rolled onto his back, his breath coming in shallow, panicked gasps. His headlamp's beam wavered, casting the creature in fragmented light.

The crimson eyes bore into him, unblinking and merciless. With a guttural roar, it leapt onto him, its weight crushing his chest. Logan screamed as its claws raked across his thigh, shredding muscle with horrifying ease. Blood sprayed across the forest floor, dark and glistening under the weak light.

"Please... stop," Logan choked, tears streaming down his face. But the creature showed no mercy.

It tore into his abdomen with a single, brutal swipe. Logan's scream pierced the night as he felt his flesh split, the searing pain unlike anything he'd ever known. His headlamp caught the sickening sight of his own insides spilling out, steam rising from the warmth of his body meeting the cold air.

The creature's maw descended, its teeth sinking into his exposed intestines. Logan's vision blurred with tears and agony as he watched it rip and devour, each bite accompanied by a sickening squelch. His hands twitched uselessly at his sides, his strength fading rapidly.

The world around him began to dim. The forest blurred, the towering trees and swirling mist fading into obscurity. But the creature's glowing eyes remained, burning into him as it fed.

Logan's breathing grew shallow, his body trembling as the cold seeped into his bones. His mind screamed at him to fight, to move, to do anything, but his body no longer obeyed. The pain began to dull, replaced by a chilling numbness. His vision tunneled, the edges going dark.

The last thing he saw was the creature lifting its bloodied maw, its crimson eyes gleaming with satisfaction as it let out a low, guttural growl. And then, the darkness claimed him.

The forest returned to its oppressive stillness, the mist swirling lazily around the trees. Logan Wright was gone, another victim claimed by the darkness.

Ghost of Gevaudan

The small room was cloaked in an oppressive stillness, the weight of unspoken truths pressing down on its occupants. John sat hunched over the table, his fingers wrapped tightly around a mug of lukewarm coffee. Beads of sweat traced jagged paths down his temples, falling into the lines etched deeply into his face. His breaths were shallow, and his gaze seemed fixed on some point beyond the worn wood of the table—beyond the here and now.

Sarah sat across from him, her notepad resting on the edge of the table, forgotten for the moment. She leaned forward slightly, her expression a mixture of concern and unease. Her knuckles whitened as she gripped her pen, her own unease mirrored in the tightness of her lips. The tension in the room was palpable, a near-tangible force that made it difficult to draw a full breath. Even Nathan, usually unflinching, shifted uneasily in his chair, his arms crossed tightly over his chest as he watched John like a predator assessing the injured.

The air was heavy, carrying the faint, bitter aroma of coffee and something else—a metallic tang, like rusted iron, that seemed to cling to the back of Sarah's throat. She swallowed hard, her eyes darting toward the window. Outside, the last rays of sunlight dipped behind the trees, painting the room in long, creeping shadows. The light bulb above flickered weakly, casting a pale, sickly glow over the table.

"You feel it, don't you?" John's voice broke the silence, raspy and low. He didn't look up. "That... weight. Like the darkness isn't just outside. Like it's here with us."

Sarah hesitated, her voice catching in her throat. "John... what happened out there?"

John's shoulders sagged further, and he wiped at his damp brow with a trembling hand. "I can't stop thinking about him. Logan." He looked up then, his eyes bloodshot and rimmed with exhaustion. "I could feel it. The fear. The way the forest… swallowed him whole."

Sarah shifted uncomfortably in her seat, a chill creeping up her spine. She opened her mouth to speak but froze as her eyes fell on the notepad in front of her. Her fingers loosened their grip on the pen, and the faint scratch of it hitting the table was the only sound in the room. The page beneath her hand was covered in jagged lines and shapes—a sketch she didn't remember drawing.

The figure was monstrous, crouched low with long, angular limbs and sharp, jagged ears. Its eyes, hollow and lifeless, seemed to exude a swirling fog. She stared at it, her pulse quickening as an unbidden wave of nausea rolled through her stomach.

"What is that?" John's voice pulled her out of her trance. He was staring at the drawing now, his expression dark and unreadable.

Sarah blinked, her mouth dry. "I… I don't know. I must've…" Her voice trailed off as Nathan stood abruptly, his chair scraping loudly against the floor. He crossed the room with purpose, leaning over Sarah's shoulder to examine the sketch.

The muscles in his jaw tightened visibly. "That…" he started, his voice low and steady, "is the Beast of Gévaudan. Or as we call it... the Ghost of Gévaudan."

Sarah's head snapped up, her brow furrowed in confusion. "What? You mean the myth? From the 1700s?"

Nathan straightened, his arms now rigid at his sides. "Not a myth," he said firmly. "Not to us."

"Us?" Sarah repeated, her voice rising slightly. She turned her attention fully to Nathan, her tone laced with incredulity. "You're saying that thing—that this—is real? How do you even know about it?"

Nathan's icy gaze met hers, unflinching. "I know more than you think," he replied flatly, his voice carrying an air of finality.

Sarah's frustration boiled over. "Who is 'we'?" she demanded, her voice sharp and demanding an answer. But Nathan didn't respond, his silence only deepening the tension.

John leaned back in his chair, his fingers tracing the rim of his mug as his eyes lingered on the drawing. "Sarah," he said, his voice softer now, "not all stories are just stories. Legends, myths… sometimes they're warnings. Records of things people tried to forget."

Sarah let out a dry laugh, the sound hollow in the tense air. "You can't be serious. What are you saying? That this—this monster is what? Hunting us? Here?"

John's gaze hardened. "I'm saying you've felt it too, haven't you? The fear. That creeping sense that something's always watching. That no matter where you go, the darkness is closer than it should be."

Sarah's face drained of color, her hand tightening on the edge of the table. "How do you know that?" she whispered.

Nathan stepped back into the shadows of the room, his tone sharp and commanding. "Sarah, we don't have time for this. Focus on what John is trying to tell you."

Her eyes flicked to him, annoyance flashing briefly before she swallowed her retort. John's voice broke the silence again, heavy and deliberate.

"There was another family," he said, his words almost a whisper. "Not just the hiker. Not just the couple. A family that came right before we were supposed to leave the reserve."

Sarah's brows knit together. "Another family? But you said…" Her voice trailed off as John's hand shook visibly, the mug rattling against the table.

"They had two kids," he said, his voice cracking. "Two boys. And a dog. They were just… they were happy. Excited for their weekend. Mark, Laura, their kids…"

Sarah reached out instinctively, placing her hand over his trembling fingers. "John," she said gently. "What happened to them?"

John closed his eyes, his lips pressed into a thin line as if willing the memories away. When he finally spoke, his voice was barely audible.

"I was there." His words hung in the air like a death knell.

Sarah's heart raced. "What do you mean, you were there?"

He opened his eyes, meeting hers with a gaze that carried the weight of unspeakable horrors. "I'll tell you everything," he said, his voice trembling. "But you have to understand… this thing, this darkness… it doesn't stop. It doesn't care. It takes, and it keeps taking."

The sun outside sank lower, its faint light casting long, twisting shadows across the room. The faint hum of distant machinery was the only sound, a stark contrast to the storm of emotions that swirled within the small space. Sarah's grip on the notepad tightened, and her pen hovered once more, ready to capture the story that was about to unfold.

Henderson Family - part 1

The crisp afternoon sunlight filtered through the dense canopy as the Henderson family—Mark, Laura, and their two sons, Jacob and Ethan—drove along the winding forest road. Their SUV was packed to the brim with gear for a weekend getaway, promising tranquility in a remote cabin deep within the wilderness. Max, their loyal German shepherd, perched between the boys in the backseat, his head occasionally popping out of the window to catch the cool breeze.

"This was a good idea," Laura said, glancing at Mark, her voice carrying a note of relief. "We really needed this."

Mark nodded, his grip steady on the wheel. "A weekend in the wild, just us and nature. The perfect present, don't you think? Feels like we haven't had enough family time lately."

Jacob, seated by the window, was only half-listening. His eyes darted toward the shadows that flitted between the towering trees. Something about the forest felt… strange. Alive, almost. He shivered slightly but kept quiet, unsure of how to describe the unease curling in his stomach.

The radio crackled suddenly, the static fading into a weather report. "…warm temperatures expected throughout the weekend, but be advised: thunderstorms are forecasted for tonight, particularly in heavily forested areas. Travelers are urged to prepare for lightning storms and potential power outages…"

Mark adjusted the volume, frowning. "Good to know. Last thing we want is to be caught off-guard by a storm out here."

Laura smiled faintly, leaning back in her seat. "A little thunder never hurt anyone. I just want to unwind."

As they rounded a bend, the trees parted briefly to reveal a small clearing where another camper was parked. A man and a woman stood outside, enjoying the afternoon sun. Mark slowed the SUV and rolled down his window.

"Hello there!" he called out, his voice friendly. "We're the Hendersons. We're headed to a cabin just up the road."

The man, who introduced himself as John, returned the greeting warmly. His wife smiled but seemed distracted, her eyes lingering on the treeline behind them. They exchanged pleasantries, discussing the beauty of the area. However, when the conversation shifted to the wildlife, John's tone grew cautious.

"There's nothing too dangerous around here," John said carefully, his words measured. "But… keep an eye on the kids and your dog. Just in case."

Mark caught the hesitation in John's voice and the way his gaze flickered back toward the forest. Was it just a general warning, or something more? He shrugged off the unease and waved goodbye as the Hendersons continued their drive toward the cabin.

Jacob's unease grew with each passing mile. The forest seemed to close in around them, the shadows between the trees growing darker, more oppressive. He kept his eyes trained on the treeline, and that's when he saw it—a large, dark shape moving swiftly between the trees. For a fleeting moment, it looked like Max, but larger, its fur darker and its eyes glowing red.

His heart stopped, and he froze in place, unable to speak. Was it real? Or was his imagination playing tricks on him?

"Mom…" he began, his voice trembling. But when he looked again, the figure was gone, swallowed by the forest. He shook his head, biting his lip. "Maybe it's nothing," he whispered to himself, though his fingers clutched the edge of his seat.

Ethan, meanwhile, was laughing as he played with Max, oblivious to Jacob's growing anxiety. However, moments later, Ethan's laughter faded. His gaze locked on the trees outside his window as something massive and fast moved through the underbrush. It ran on two legs but hunched low, its speed and power unnerving.

"Did you see that?" Ethan asked in a hushed voice, turning to Jacob.

Jacob shook his head but clenched his fists. He didn't want to admit what he'd seen earlier. Both boys sat in tense silence for the remainder of the drive, unspoken fears bubbling just beneath the surface.

The Hendersons arrived at the cabin just as the sun dipped lower in the sky, casting the forest in deep golden hues. Jacob and Ethan eagerly jumped out of the car, Max darting off toward the trees with his nose to the ground. The boys' excitement was infectious, and for a moment, the earlier tension faded.

"Stay close to the cabin!" Laura called after them, her smile broad as she watched them explore the clearing.

Mark began unloading the SUV, but his movements slowed when Max returned, his ears pinned back and his posture tense. The dog's usual exuberance was gone, replaced by a cautious demeanor that sent a chill down Mark's spine.

"What's wrong, boy?" he murmured, kneeling to scratch Max behind the ears. The dog didn't respond, his gaze fixed on the treeline as he let out a low, wary growl.

Inside the cabin, the family quickly settled in. Laura set about arranging their things while Mark double-checked their supplies. Ethan pulled out his drawing pad and began sketching at the table, his tongue poking out slightly as he concentrated.

"What're you drawing, buddy?" Laura asked, pausing to admire his work.

Ethan held up the page proudly. "It's us! See? That's the car, and that's Max. And those are the trees."

Laura smiled, but her expression faltered when she noticed the figure looming behind the SUV in the drawing. It was massive, its tall, angular shape dark and menacing. Two glowing red eyes stared out from the sketch, their intensity almost leaping off the page.

"And who's this?" she asked, pointing at the figure.

Ethan shrugged, his tone nonchalant. "I don't know. Just something I saw."

Laura's heart skipped a beat. She forced a smile and ruffled Ethan's hair before glancing toward the window, her unease returning tenfold. Something wasn't right. She could feel it now, too.

As the sun dipped behind the horizon, the forest's earlier vibrancy gave way to an oppressive darkness. The family ate dinner by the light of the cabin's modest fixtures, but the mood had shifted. Even the boys' playful banter felt subdued.

After the kids were tucked into bed, Laura sat at the kitchen table, her hands wrapped around a mug of tea. Mark joined her, the warmth of his coffee doing little to ease the chill that had settled in his bones.

"That drawing Ethan made…" Laura began, her voice barely above a whisper. "It's been bothering me."

Mark sighed, running a hand through his hair. "It's just a drawing, Laura. Kids have wild imaginations."

"Wild imagination doesn't explain those eyes," she countered. "Or the way Max has been acting. Something's out there, Mark."

He opened his mouth to respond, but a low, guttural growl from Max cut him off. The dog stood near the front door, his ears flat and his teeth bared. His gaze was locked on the window, his body rigid with tension.

“Mark,” Laura whispered, fear creeping into her voice. “Max senses something.”

Mark rose from his chair, his movements slow and deliberate. “Stay here. I’ll check outside.”

As he grabbed a flashlight from the counter, the lights in the cabin flickered once, twice, and then went out entirely, plunging them into darkness.

Henderson Family - part 2

Mark muttered under his breath, his hands fumbling for the flashlight on the counter. The cabin's sudden plunge into darkness had rattled him more than he wanted to admit.

"What the hell?"

Laura stood nearby, her voice strained. "Mark, the power's out."

"I know," he replied, flicking the flashlight on and sweeping its beam across the room. "It's probably just the storm they mentioned on the radio."

But Laura's gut told her otherwise. Her unease was palpable, a knot tightening in her chest. "Go check the fuse box," she urged, her voice tinged with worry.

Mark nodded, grabbing a jacket and heading for the door. The moment he stepped outside, a wave of oppressive silence hit him like a wall. The air was thick and damp, suffused with a strange, electric charge. The forest, usually alive with chirps and rustling leaves, was utterly still. It felt wrong—as if the entire world was holding its breath.

Mark's flashlight wavered slightly in his grip as he moved toward the side of the cabin. He scanned the treeline, his skin prickling. For a fleeting moment, he thought he heard something—a faint, almost imperceptible breath behind him. He spun around, the flashlight's beam slicing through the darkness. Nothing. Only shadows and the suffocating quiet of the forest.

Forcing himself to focus, he aimed the light at the fuse box. His stomach dropped. The cables had been cleanly cut, their frayed ends sparking faintly in the damp air. His heartbeat quickened, adrenaline coursing through his veins. This wasn't an accident. Someone—or something—had done this.

He bolted back inside, his voice tight with urgency. "Laura, something's wrong. The cables have been cut."

Laura's heart raced. She darted to the boys' room, her maternal instincts kicking into overdrive. Jacob was already standing by the window, his small frame silhouetted against the glass. His eyes were wide, reflecting a terror no child should ever feel.

"Mom," he whispered, his voice trembling. "There's something out there."

Laura knelt beside him, placing a protective arm around his shoulders. "What did you see?" she asked, her voice barely above a whisper.

Jacob hesitated, his gaze fixed on the darkness beyond the window. "Something sharp," he finally said. "It tapped on the glass. I heard footsteps... and breathing."

Laura hugged him tightly, trying to steady her own trembling hands. "It's alright, baby. We're safe in here." But even as she spoke the words, they rang hollow in her ears. Max, their loyal German shepherd, stood rigid by the door, his hackles raised and a deep, guttural growl rumbling from his throat. He knew something they didn't.

Meanwhile, Mark made his way toward the car. His gut churned with a sickening mix of dread and determination. As he approached the vehicle, his flashlight flickered, casting erratic shadows across the gravel. A faint rustling sound from the woods made him freeze. Was it the wind? Or something else? His grip tightened on the flashlight as he forced himself forward.

When he reached the car, his worst fears were confirmed. The hood was slightly ajar. Mark's hands shook as he lifted it, revealing the battery cables, torn apart in the same precise manner as the fuse box wires. His breath hitched. This wasn't just sabotage; it was calculated.

A sudden crash from inside the cabin shattered the stillness. Max's frantic barking was followed by Laura's scream, sharp and filled with raw terror. Then came the boys' voices, crying out for their father.

Panic surged through Mark as he sprinted back toward the cabin, but he barely made it halfway before something massive slammed into him, sending him sprawling to the ground. He hit the earth hard, the impact knocking the wind from his lungs. Pain seared through his leg, and when he looked down, his jeans were soaked with blood from a deep, jagged gash across his thigh.

Dazed and gasping, Mark tried to push himself up, but his body betrayed him. He could hear the chaos inside the cabin: Max's desperate growls turning into pained whimpers, Laura's screams cutting through the night, and the boys sobbing in sheer terror.

Mark's vision blurred as he began to crawl, his body dragging painfully across the rough ground. The cold, damp earth clung to him, but the searing agony in his heart was far worse. He had to get to them. He had to save them.

As he drew closer to the cabin, he caught a horrifying glimpse through the window. A grotesque silhouette towered over his family. The creature's massive frame pressed their bodies against the glass, its crimson eyes burning with malice.

"Mark, help us!" Laura's voice cracked with desperation. She clutched Jacob tightly, her face streaked with tears and blood. But her plea was cut short as the beast's jaws clamped down on her shoulder, tearing through flesh and bone with sickening ease. Blood sprayed across the window, thick and dark, obscuring the scene inside.

Mark froze, his body paralyzed with shock. This couldn't be real. It had to be a nightmare. He blinked rapidly, willing himself to wake up, but the horrific tableau before him remained.

Inside, Laura turned to Jacob, her voice a trembling whisper. "Close your eyes, sweetheart. It'll be over soon. Mommy and Daddy... love you..."

The beast's jaws found Jacob next, tearing into the boy's small arm as his screams pierced the night. Mark's mind shattered under the weight of the moment. Tears streamed down his face as he tried to crawl faster, but his body refused to obey.

With a final, agonized scream, blood erupted across the window, coating it entirely. The sound of bones snapping and flesh ripping filled the air, a macabre symphony that would haunt Mark forever. And then, the beast pulled them away from the window, disappearing into the shadows with its prey.

The cabin fell silent, save for the faint crackle of broken glass and Mark's ragged, uneven breathing. He lay there, helpless, as the fog began to roll in, swallowing the cabin and its horrific secrets. Through the mist, he could barely make out the blood-streaked window, now devoid of life.

The pain in his leg was excruciating, but the agony in his soul was far worse. He had failed them. His family was gone, and he was powerless to stop it. Tears blurred his vision as his body gave out, collapsing against the cold, unforgiving ground.

Somewhere in the distance, a faint rustling broke the oppressive silence. Mark's head turned weakly, his breath hitching. Was it the creature, returning to finish him off? Or was it something else—a sign that the forest wasn't done with him yet?

The silence that followed was suffocating, pressing down on him like a weight he could never lift. The last of the creature's footsteps faded into the distance, but Mark knew it wasn't gone. It was out there, lurking, waiting.

And he was all alone.

Shattered Sanctuary - part 1

"I had planned to take a hike through the woods, heading toward the cabin area. Henderson passed through yesterday afternoon and had booked one of the cabins. They had kids, so I thought maybe they might need something. I packed a few things in my backpack, along with a flashlight in case it got dark before I could return. I asked Lucas if he wanted to come along, but… you know how kids are. He was more interested in playing with my phone, the only one we had with us. I let him keep it."

John paused, glancing down at his scarred hands, the deep scratches a vivid reminder. The weight of what had happened hung heavily on him.

"I went back inside the camper to say goodbye to Erika, kissed Jacob on the forehead. My wife stood at the door, smiling. 'John, be careful,' she said with a wink, then kissed me and hugged me. Erika… she watched me with sad eyes, always a daddy's girl. You could see it in her face."

Swallowing hard, John struggled to keep his voice steady. "My wife closed the door, and that was the last time I saw them alive."

The air had been thick that day. "The hike wasn't bad at first," John continued. "Until I made my way up the hill. The ground beneath my feet was uneven and steep. I made it to the coniferous forest; it was dense, the trees packed tightly together, their branches clawing at me as I struggled to get through. The damp pine needles made the ascent even harder, my boots slipping with every step."

The sun barely pierced through the trees, and it was quiet—too quiet. No birds, no breeze, just an unsettling silence.

John's voice grew lower as the memory crept back. "I came to a dense patch of trees, and that's when I saw them. Tracks. At first, I thought they were bear prints, but they were too big—five toes, claws deeply embedded in the mud. Whatever made them wasn't a bear. They led toward the cabins, so I followed."

He hesitated, his heart beginning to race. "Could it be hunting?" He shook off the thought, but the fear lingered. "I should have turned back then. I should have gone home."

John paused, gathering himself. Shaking slightly, he continued, "The sun was setting, the air thick, but I kept going. I jogged toward the cabins. That's when I saw their car, parked right in front."

The car's hood was open, the battery cables severed cleanly. Something deliberate had done this. John's pulse quickened. The air felt thick, like it was pressing in on him from all sides. The door to the cabin was ajar, gently swaying in the breeze. The sight of it made his stomach drop.

"Is anyone here?" he called, but the silence swallowed his words.

He moved toward the entrance, each step growing heavier, dread building in his chest.

The living room was in shambles—furniture overturned, deep claw marks raked across the walls. His breathing grew shallow. Something had torn through this place with intent. This wasn't a random attack.

He moved further inside, every fiber of his being screaming to turn back. But he couldn't—not without knowing.

The nauseating stench of decay hit him as he reached the staircase, the foul air growing thicker with every step up. His heart hammered as he neared the top.

The smell. God, the smell.

Then, he saw Max. The poor dog, pinned to the floor, skewered by a wooden beam. His fur matted with blood, his body covered in deep, vicious wounds. John choked back the bile rising in his throat. Max had tried to protect them. But it hadn't been enough.

His legs trembled as he reached the bedroom door, half-closed. He pushed it open, and his world shattered.

The mother lay across the bed, her body twisted, trying to shield her children. Blood soaked the sheets, smeared across the window. Her throat and shoulder were torn apart, massive bite marks carved into her flesh. One of her legs was barely recognizable—shredded and torn to pieces.

The boys lay nearby. One missing an arm, his chest torn open, his face mangled. The other child was half under the bed, his body flayed, skin stripped away, his small frame broken and torn apart.

John staggered back, gasping, unable to comprehend the horror in front of him. His legs nearly gave out beneath him. He had to get out of there. Now.

As he rushed down the stairs, the sickening stench of death clung to his senses. The oppressive silence outside sent chills down his spine, his legs nearly buckling under the weight of fear. He burst out the door, his breath coming in ragged gasps, and then he saw Mark. Bruised and bloodied, stumbling through the mist.

"Mark!" he called out, running toward him.

Mark's eyes were wild with terror, his body trembling. "It's coming… it's coming," he screamed, pointing back toward the cabin. John grabbed him by the shoulders, trying to calm him down, but Mark's words were frantic, barely coherent.

"We need to go, now!" John urged, pulling him with him.

But before they could even take another step, the ground trembled under them, the heavy thud of something large approaching through the fog. The earth seemed to pulse with every step it took, the vibration crawling up John's spine like an electric shock.

Mark froze, his face pale, his eyes locked onto the looming shadow that grew larger with each step. "Run!" he screamed, breaking free from John's grasp and sprinting into the trees.

John barely had time to react before the massive silhouette of the creature emerged from the fog, its glowing eyes fixed on them. His stomach twisted into a knot as he saw the monstrous form reach out for Mark. Mark's scream echoed through the night as the beast's claws slashed through the air, his body disappearing into the fog.

John dove into the underbrush, heart racing, body trembling as he pressed himself flat against the ground. The fog was thick around him, muffling every sound. The sickening crunch of bones breaking echoed through the mist as the beast tore into Mark's remains.

His breath caught in his throat. He couldn't scream. He couldn't move. It was too close. If he made a sound, it would find him next.

John lay there, every muscle tense, his pulse pounding in his ears. Thoughts of his family overwhelmed him. What if the creature was already hunting them? What if he was too late? He forced himself up, his body trembling as he sprinted through the suffocating gloom of the forest.

Keep moving. Don't stop. Don't think. Just run.

Branches whipped against his face as he stumbled forward, the cold air clawing at his skin. Fear crawled up his spine, as if something unseen was just behind him, ready to strike. But he couldn't stop. He wouldn't stop. His family needed him.

As John's voice cracked, the room fell silent. Sarah's pen hovered over her notepad, her hand trembling as she struggled to process his words. Nathan sat in the corner, his jaw tight, his eyes cold and unyielding.

John's final words cut through the silence like a blade. "I'll never forget the sound. The sound of it tearing him apart."

Shattered Sanctuary - part 2

I lay there, every muscle tense, my pulse pounding in my ears. Thoughts of my family overwhelmed me. What if the creature was already hunting them? What if I was too late? My breath came in ragged gasps as I forced myself to move, limbs trembling with fear and exhaustion.

Branches whipped against my face as I tore through the suffocating gloom of the forest. Keep moving. Don't stop. Don't think. Just run. The icy air clawed at my skin, burning my lungs with every breath. Fear crept along my spine, as if unseen claws hovered inches from my back. The memory of what I'd witnessed clawed at my mind, refusing to let go. Is it following me? Is it waiting to strike?

I'd seen predators before, even large ones, but this was different. Nothing about it was natural. Its raw, terrifying power had been burned into my mind. Each step felt like running toward an abyss. I glanced over my shoulder, the shadows behind me twisting like ghostly specters.

I have to keep going. Don't look back. Don't stop. Their faces flashed before my eyes—Erika, Lucas, Jacob. They need me. I can't fail them.

I staggered to a halt, gasping for air, the cold cutting through my throat like shards of glass. My legs quivered beneath me, adrenaline burning through my veins. I wasn't easily shaken, but this... this was different. This felt like something ripped straight from the depths of hell.

BANG!

The deafening crash jolted me, and I hit the ground hard. I crawled toward a tree, the rough bark tearing at my hands. My only thought was survival.

Another crash echoed through the forest, closer this time. Was it the creature? Was it hunting me? My heart hammered violently. Move. I have to keep moving.

A flash of lightning split the sky, illuminating the chaos around me. The forest seemed to shift and shudder, alive in the flickering light. And then a sickening realization gripped me, paralyzing in its clarity: What if it's already there? What if I'm too late?

I forced my aching body to move, driven by sheer desperation. Every step was agony, but stopping wasn't an option. It's out here, somewhere. I can feel it. But I have to reach them first. I can't stop now.

At the top of a steep hill, I paused, panting, my breath clouding in the freezing air. Below, about 500 meters away, a faint flicker of firelight caught my eye—a fragile beacon against the oppressive darkness. Shadows danced in the dim glow as the mist thickened, swirling like ghostly tendrils. I took a shaky step forward, but my foot caught on a root hidden in the underbrush, sending me tumbling down the slope.

Pain shot through my body as I hit the ground. The world spun around me, but I pushed myself up. Rain began to fall, cold droplets stinging my skin like needles.

I can't stop now.

I fumbled for my flashlight, its trembling beam slicing through the darkness. My pants were torn, but I'd managed to avoid any major injuries. Then I saw it—a deep gash on my arm, blood trickling down and mixing with the rain. There was no time to stop. No time to think.

A guttural growl pierced the night, low and menacing, vibrating through my chest. My heart seized in terror. It wasn't thunder. It was close. Too close. The camp was just ahead, and it was hunting. I had to move. Now.

Stumbling through the downpour, every step felt heavier, like dragging myself through a waking nightmare. My clothes clung to my body, soaked and freezing. The forest blurred around me, a chaotic swirl of dark shapes and shadows. I tripped, nearly crashing into the campfire's glow. There, in the flickering light, I saw him—Lucas. My boy.

He stood with his back to me, oblivious to the rain or the suffocating darkness. Panic surged through me. My hands fumbled for the car keys, but they slipped from my grasp, disappearing into the mud.

"No! Not now!" I shouted, digging frantically through the muck, my fingers numb and trembling. Each heartbeat thundered in my ears, drowning out the storm. My vision blurred, panic threatening to consume me. Finally, my fingers closed around the keys. I jammed them into the lock, throwing open the trunk.

Inside, under a hastily thrown blanket, lay the weapon chest. My hands shook as I ripped it open, loading the last five shells into the rifle. My mind raced as I slammed the trunk shut. My boy hadn't moved. The rain stopped, and silence fell like a death shroud.

The firelight illuminated a shadow, low and creeping toward Lucas on all fours. My heart plummeted. My breath caught in my throat as I flicked the safety off with a trembling hand. The sharp click shattered the quiet.

The creature froze.

It rose slowly, unfolding to its full height, its monstrous silhouette looming against the firelight. Steam curled from its open maw as it stared at Lucas. He pulled an earbud from his ear, turning to face the shadow. He froze, his eyes widening in terror.

"RUN!" I screamed, my voice cracking under the weight of desperation. "Please, for God's sake, RUN!"

Lucas jumped at the sound of my voice, his face a mask of confusion and fear. The creature tilted its head, its gaze piercing, intelligent. It looked at me, then back at Lucas, almost taunting. Saliva dripped from its maw, sizzling as it hit the wet ground.

"Run inside when I count to three!" I shouted, my voice trembling. "One..."

The creature's lips curled back, revealing jagged teeth. Its growl rumbled like distant thunder.

“Two...”

The beast crouched, muscles coiling.

“Three!”

I raised the rifle and fired. The shot rang out, but the creature moved too fast. Lucas screamed as it swiped at him, sending him hurtling into the side of the camper. My heart shattered as I saw his limp body crumple against the door.

“BANG!” I fired again, the bullet grazing its neck. It roared, the sound primal and earth-shattering. It turned its attention to me.

Before I could react, the beast lunged. Its claws struck me like a freight train, flinging me into a tree. Pain exploded through my body as I hit the ground. My rifle lay meters away, just out of reach. My vision blurred, rain mixing with blood as I struggled to crawl toward it.

The fire crackled weakly, the only sound in the sudden, oppressive silence. I reached for the rifle, my fingers brushing against the barrel. Warm breath pooled against the back of my neck.

I froze.

A low, guttural growl vibrated against my skin. Claws pressed into my back, their tips slicing through fabric and flesh. My fingers locked in terror. I felt the weight of it, the heat of its breath, the inescapable finality of the moment.

The air swirled, thick and suffocating. And then—

BANG.

Everything went black.

The death Trap - Part 1

Silence. The caravan was cloaked in a suffocating stillness, broken only by the sound of Emily's shallow breaths. Erika clung to her mother, trembling, as if unseen eyes bore down on them from the darkness. Emily's mind raced, trying to suppress the rising panic. She had never felt so vulnerable, so exposed.

"Mom, what is it?" Erika's whisper was barely audible, her voice trembling.

Emily swallowed hard, her hands gripping the edge of the table. "I don't know," she admitted, her gaze flicking toward the window. She was terrified to look too long, afraid of what she might see.

Their whispers were interrupted by a faint beeping from the wildlife alarm. The sharp, repetitive sound cut through the air like a warning bell. Erika let out a small scream, clamping her hands over her ears.

"Shhh, it will be okay," Emily urged, trying to sound convincing. But the crack in her voice betrayed her. The air felt heavy, charged with a menace that was almost tangible. She could feel it in her chest, a pressure that refused to let her breathe deeply.

Suddenly, there was a light tapping, sharp and deliberate, against the glass. Tap. Tap. Tap. It circled the caravan, the noise moving from one window to another. Erika's eyes widened, tears spilling down her cheeks.

"It's searching," she whispered, her voice breaking. "Mom, it's looking for us."

Emily hugged her tightly, her heart pounding. "Please, darling, try to breathe. Don't wake Jacob," she whispered. Her mind raced for a plan, but there was none. The caravan felt like a tin can, fragile and vulnerable against whatever was out there.

A sudden scraping sound erupted outside, loud and jarring. The entire caravan rocked under the force, the lights flickering once before dying completely. Darkness swallowed them.

"Oh my God," Erika gasped, her voice barely more than a breath. The icy grip of fear tightened around Emily's chest. It was intelligent. Whatever was out there wasn't just a beast. It was trying to terrify them, and it was succeeding.

The thought was interrupted by Erika's pale, ghost-like face. "Mom, look," she whispered, pointing toward the rear window.

Emily's blood turned to ice as her gaze followed her daughter's trembling finger. There, pressed against the glass, was a massive hand. Long, black claws scratched faintly at the surface, leaving deep grooves in the glass. Heavy footsteps echoed outside, each one sending vibrations through the floor. The ground trembled under the weight of whatever stalked them.

Suddenly, the door to the caravan slammed shut. The sound was deafening, final. Erika let out a sob, her small body shaking uncontrollably.

“It’s trying to get in!” Erika screamed, clutching at her mother.

Emily’s breath caught in her throat. She’d locked the door after the attack on her husband and Lucas. What had happened to them? Were they even still alive? Her mind spun with questions she didn’t want to answer.

Glancing back at the rear window, her heart sank further. Two red eyes glowed in the darkness, burning through the glass like twin embers. They pierced her soul, a gaze so predatory it felt like a physical assault. Emily froze, her body trembling.

“Hide!” she whispered urgently to Erika, her voice trembling with fear.

“Why?” Erika sobbed, clutching at her mother’s arm.

“Because I say so,” Emily snapped, her voice shaking. She forced herself to stay calm, to be strong for her daughter. “Whatever you do, don’t come out, no matter what you hear!”

Erika nodded, tears streaming down her face. She crawled into a nearby cupboard, closing the door behind her. Her sobs were muffled, her prayers silent as she begged for the creature not to find her little brother.

The tapping stopped. The silence that followed was deafening. Then, with a sudden crash, the rear window shattered. Glass shards exploded into the caravan, cutting into Emily’s face. The cold air rushed in like a tidal wave, chilling her to the bone. She opened her eyes, blood trickling down her cheek, and saw two massive hands pressing down on the caravan. Claws dug into the bed frame, splintering the wood.

Her breath caught as the creature's head appeared. It was enormous, dog-like but twisted, its skin covered in coarse black fur with red-tipped ends. The eyes glowed brighter now, searing into her with malevolent intelligence. Its jagged teeth glinted in the dim light, saliva dripping onto the bedspread. The stench of rotten meat and wet fur filled the air, making her gag.

Emily's hand crept toward the drawer beneath the table. Her husband's revolver was there, her only hope. She moved slowly, her every nerve on edge as the creature growled low in its throat. Its breath steamed in the cold air, each exhale like a predator savoring its prey.

Her fingers found the handle of the revolver. She seized it, throwing it up and firing. BANG! BANG! BANG! The deafening shots rang out, but the creature barely flinched. It turned its head toward her, those red eyes locking onto hers with a mocking gaze. It was toying with her, confident, unshaken.

Then Jacob screamed.

Emily's heart shattered. The creature turned toward the curtain where her youngest hid. It sniffed the air, its massive jaws twitching as it slowly pushed its head past the fabric.

"NO!" Emily screamed, her voice raw with desperation. She fired again, but the creature didn't stop. It yanked the curtain aside, revealing her terrified son.

Time seemed to freeze. Emily's trembling voice broke the silence. "I'm so sorry, Jacob," she whispered, her tears falling freely. She raised the revolver, her hands shaking uncontrollably.

BANG.

The gunshot echoed through the caravan, silencing Jacob's screams. Emily's breath hitched, her heart breaking into a thousand pieces. She had killed her son. She had saved him from a fate worse than death, but the weight of what she had done crushed her.

The creature dropped Jacob's lifeless body, the small frame hitting the floor with a sickening thud. It leaned down, sniffing the blood-soaked corpse. Then, with chilling satisfaction, it licked the blood from its claws. Its gaze returned to Emily, a cold, malevolent hunger burning in its eyes.

The death Trap - Part 2

The mother pressed herself against the caravan wall, her body trembling violently as panic overwhelmed her. Her breath came in shallow, broken gasps. “John!” she screamed, her voice cracking with desperation. “Help us! Where are you?” Sobs racked her body, raw and primal, as the horrifying reality of their situation settled in. Deep down, she knew—this was the end.

Beneath the caravan, John stirred. His mind was a fog of pain and confusion. The left side of his head throbbed, swollen and bleeding, the sticky warmth of blood trickling down his temple. Groaning, he forced his eyes open, disoriented. “Where…?” he muttered, his voice weak. Pain radiated through his body, pinning him down against the cold, sticky mud. It seeped into his pores, numbing his limbs. He shuddered as the freezing night air filled his lungs, each breath visible in weak, trembling puffs.

Panic hit him like a lightning strike. “Lucas…” he whispered hoarsely, the memory of his son flashing before his eyes. He willed his body to move, ignoring the fiery protest of his muscles. The sticky mud clung to him as he clawed at the ground, his trembling hands searching for something to grip. Around him, the world was eerily quiet. The campfire’s glow flickered faintly in the distance, casting ghostly shadows in the surrounding darkness.

Then—CRACK! The deafening sound of a gunshot split the air, leaving his ears ringing. His heart raced as he heard Emily’s voice—raw, trembling, filled with despair. She was pleading for her life.

The beast was closing in, its massive silhouette casting an ominous shadow across the caravan. For a moment, it paused, sniffing the air. Emily's heart stopped as its glowing eyes shifted toward the cupboards. A wave of terror crashed over her—it knew. It knew where Erika was hiding.

"No," she whispered, her voice barely audible, her hands trembling. "No… please…"

Without warning, the creature lunged, tearing through the wood with monstrous strength. Erika's scream cut through the air as the beast yanked her from the cupboard. The sickening crunch of her arm snapping reverberated in the small space, the sound filling her mother's ears like a death knell.

"Please!" Emily cried, her voice raw with desperation. "I'm begging you—let her go! Please, with all my heart…"

The monster turned its glowing eyes toward Emily, its expression unreadable, but its intent unmistakable. Erika whimpered in its grip, tears streaming down her pale, terrified face. Emily's shaking hand reached for the revolver, her fingers fumbling as she raised it. She aimed it at Erika, her vision blurred with tears.

"Forgive me," she whispered. Click. The empty chamber echoed like a death sentence.

Emily's heart shattered. She had no bullets left. The creature snarled, its grotesque jaws snapping as it tightened its grip on Erika. In one horrifying motion, it tore her arm from her body. Blood sprayed across the walls, the sound of bone snapping filling the air. Erika's screams pierced the night, a soul-shattering cry of agony and terror.

John, trapped beneath the caravan, heard every sound. His wife's desperate cries, Erika's blood-curdling screams—they were knives twisting in his soul. Tears streamed down his mud-streaked face as he struggled in vain to free himself.

"Daddy!" Erika's broken voice cried out, her final plea for help. The creature's monstrous jaws descended, sinking into her small, fragile body. Blood poured from the horrific wounds as the beast tore into her, piece by piece. Her trembling fingers twitched, a final, desperate movement before the life drained from her.

With her last breath, she whispered, "Daddy…"

And then, silence.

Emily stared at her daughter's mangled, lifeless body, frozen in place by grief and horror. Erika's once-beautiful face was unrecognizable, her back ripped open, her ribs exposed. Her long, golden hair, now drenched in blood, clung to her broken form.

The monster turned its gaze to Emily. Its glowing eyes locked onto hers, a sinister hunger radiating from them. Blood dripped from its jaws, the remnants of Erika's body still dangling from its jagged teeth. The stench of decay filled the air, suffocating her. She felt bile rise in her throat, her stomach twisting as the creature savored her terror.

John, beneath the caravan, could only listen as Emily's sobs echoed above him. "John..." her voice broke. "I'm sorry. I couldn't protect them... they're gone."

Her words tore through him like a blade. His chest heaved, but no air filled his lungs. He clawed at the mud, his fingers bloody and raw. He wanted to scream, to beg the creature to take him instead, but his voice failed him.

The caravan creaked ominously as the beast shifted its weight. Its claws scraped against the metal, slow and deliberate, drawing out every agonizing second. Emily's sobs grew quieter, her voice trembling with resignation. "John, I love you. Tell Lucas... I'm sorry."

"No!" John's voice erupted in a raw, desperate cry. "Emily, fight! Please, fight!"

Another crash shook the caravan. The beast snarled, and Emily's cries turned to muffled screams. The wet, sickening sound of flesh tearing filled the air as the creature feasted. John's heart shattered with every sound, his screams turning to anguished sobs.

And then, the beast stopped. It let out a deep, guttural growl, its menace vibrating through the ground. The caravan shook violently as it leapt through the shattered window, disappearing into the forest.

For a moment, there was only silence. John lay in the mud, his body trembling, his mind consumed by grief.

Then, realization hit him like a bolt of lightning.

“Lucas,” he gasped, his voice a broken whisper. His son—his only remaining family—was still out there. And the beast was hunting him.

Summoning every ounce of strength, John roared into the night. “Run, Lucas! Run! Don’t stop!”

The forest swallowed his words, the darkness pressing in like a suffocating blanket. John collapsed, tears streaming down his face, as the echoes of his screams faded into the void.

Chapter: 9-1-1

The forest swallowed Lucas whole. Towering trees loomed like twisted giants, their skeletal branches clawing at the stormy sky. Rain slipped through the canopy, striking the ground in a relentless rhythm. But Lucas barely noticed the wet chill soaking through his clothes.

All he could hear was his father's desperate shout echoing in his mind:

"Run, Lucas! Don't stop! Run for your life!"

The words had burned into his brain, and they pushed him forward now, even as his legs threatened to collapse beneath him. His breath came in jagged gasps, clouds of steam in the icy air. Mud clung to his shoes, pulling him back with every frantic step. Branches lashed at his face, slicing his skin, but the pain was distant—nothing compared to the ache in his chest.

Somewhere behind him, far but not far enough, he could still hear the faint echoes of screams. His mother. His sister. Each cry was a shard of glass piercing his heart.

"I have to get help," he told himself. His hand tightened around the glowing phone, its faint light a fragile beacon in the endless dark.

A soft ping.

2% battery remaining.

“No... no, please,” he whispered, his voice shaking. He stumbled to a halt, his feet skidding in the wet earth. His fingers trembled as he wiped the screen with his sleeve, smearing dirt and water across the glass. The faint light flickered, and for a moment, he thought it would die completely.

Then he saw it: one bar of signal.

Lucas let out a choked sob of relief, tears mingling with the rain on his face. His fingers fumbled across the keypad, slipping as he pressed 9-1-1. The phone rang, and every second felt like a lifetime.

The forest was silent now. Too silent. Even the rain seemed muted, absorbed by the mud and leaves. Lucas could feel the stillness pressing in, the suffocating weight of eyes watching him.

"Pick up. Please, pick up," he whispered, his voice cracking with desperation.

The ringing stopped.

"911, what is your emergency?"

The voice startled him—it was soft, calm, almost motherly. For a moment, Lucas couldn’t speak. His breath hitched, and he stared at the screen as if the voice might reach through it and pull him to safety.

"Hello? Are you there? Can you tell me what’s wrong?"

Lucas squeezed his eyes shut, his lips trembling. “Help,” he croaked, barely a whisper.

"It’s okay, sweetheart. Take a deep breath and tell me what’s happening. What’s your name?"

“L-Lucas,” he stammered, his voice trembling.

“Hi, Lucas. My name is Sandra, and I’m here to help you. Can you tell me what’s going on?”

Lucas gasped for air, clutching the phone like a lifeline. “We... we need help! Please!” he cried. His voice cracked as the words spilled out, fast and raw. “Something attacked us—my dad and me—and my mom and sister—” His voice faltered, breaking on a sob. “She screamed! I think it killed her! It’s still out there!”

Sandra’s voice remained steady, though Lucas could hear the faint edge of urgency creeping in. “You’re doing great, Lucas. Are you by yourself right now?”

“I don’t know!” Lucas cried. “My sister—she’s gone! My mom too—I think it got them! My dad’s hurt! He told me to run!”

“You were so brave to run for help, Lucas,” Sandra said gently. “Can you tell me where you are? Do you see anything that could help us find you?”

“I don’t know! It’s just trees! It all looks the same!”

The phone pinged again.

1% battery remaining.

Lucas let out a sob, the sound ragged and broken. “It’s going to die,” he whispered.

“Stay with me, Lucas. Just hold on, okay? We’re going to find you,” Sandra promised, her voice still calm, though Lucas could hear the strain in it now.

Then it came.

A low rumble, deep and guttural, rolled through the earth. Lucas froze, his breath catching in his throat. The sound started as a faint vibration but grew louder, heavier, until it shook the ground beneath him. He could feel it in his chest, a primal force that made every instinct in his body scream to run.

“Oh no. No, no, no,” Lucas whimpered, his knees buckling.

“Lucas?” Sandra’s voice rose. “Lucas, talk to me! What’s happening?”

“It’s here,” Lucas whispered, tears streaming down his face. “Oh God, it’s here.”

“What’s here, Lucas? Who’s there?”

The shadows shifted. Between the trees, two glowing eyes blinked to life, red as embers. They moved closer, burning brighter, until Lucas could see the massive outline of the beast.

The growl deepened, a rumbling snarl that filled the air with menace. The stench hit him—thick, metallic, like blood and decay. Lucas stumbled back, his breath hitching in shallow gasps.

"Help me!" he screamed, his voice breaking.

"I'm trying, Lucas!" Sandra's voice cracked with panic. "Just keep moving! We're locating your phone!"

But it was too late.

The beast exploded from the shadows, its hulking form ripping through the trees like paper. Lucas screamed as it lunged for him, its glowing eyes the last thing he saw.

The phone tumbled from his hand, landing in the mud. Sandra could only listen as chaos erupted—branches snapping, wet, heavy thuds, Lucas' screams echoing, desperate and raw.

"LUCAS?! LUCAS?!" she shouted into the headset.

The roar that followed was unlike anything she had ever heard—low, guttural, primal. Lucas' cries grew weaker, fainter, until they were nothing but wet, choking gasps.

Then—silence.

Sandra sat frozen in her chair, her hands shaking. “Lucas?” she whispered.

The line clicked, and a new voice cut through the static. Calm. Cold.

“Hello, Sandra. We’ll take it from here.”

Her wide eyes darted to the screen. Words began to scroll across it:

Satellite location... Phone located... Asset found... Phantom Activated.

Her voice cracked. “What the hell is happening?”

The Rescue

The forest swallowed John whole. Cold mud pressed against his face, seeping into his pores and filling his nostrils with the putrid mix of damp earth and blood. Every muscle in his body screamed with pain, but none of it compared to the gaping void in his chest. His wife's desperate cries and Erika's final, broken plea echoed endlessly in his mind.

Daddy!

The word tore at his soul, each syllable another knife twisting in his gut. He had failed them all—his wife, his daughter, and Lucas. The thought of his son running blindly into the darkness left him choking on his own despair. "I'm sorry," he whispered to no one, the words swallowed by the oppressive silence. "I'm so sorry."

Rain pelted the forest canopy above, droplets sliding down twisted branches and striking the ground in relentless rhythm. The cold seeped through John's soaked clothes, numbing his broken body. He wanted to move, to stand, but the weight of failure pinned him down, as if the forest itself was punishing him.

"Come and take me!" he bellowed hoarsely into the void. "You took them! You took everything! Just finish it!"

His voice echoed into nothingness, met only with the oppressive stillness of the woods. He buried his face in the mud, his sobs muffled by the earth. Every breath he took was shallow, sharp, and uneven, his body barely clinging to life.

Then, a faint vibration rippled through the ground beneath him. Subtle at first, it grew louder, accompanied by a rhythmic hum that sliced through the rain. John's breath hitched. The sound was mechanical, alien in the natural world. Rotor blades. The vibrations grew stronger, the ground trembling beneath their power.

John forced his eyes open, blinking away the mud and tears. Blinding beams of light cut through the darkness, sweeping across the campsite. He saw it all in stark clarity: the mangled wreckage of the camper, blood pooling in the dirt, and fragments of the life he'd once known scattered like debris.

Erika's scarf fluttered in the wind, caught on a jagged piece of metal. A child's toy lay half-buried in the mud, its bright colors dulled by grime. John shut his eyes tightly, his heart twisting. He couldn't bear to look.

"MZOs deployed," a voice crackled through the air, its tone calm yet commanding. The words meant nothing to John, who lay motionless as the vibrations intensified. Small, spherical devices scattered around him, their blinking green lights casting eerie glows across the ground. The hum of technology filled the air, alien and precise.

And then came the thud.

Heavy, deliberate footsteps crushed the mud beyond the camper. John's eyes flickered open, his vision blurred. Through the blinding beams of light, he saw them: silhouettes cloaked in armor, their visors reflecting the forest's shadows. They moved with precision, weapons scanning the perimeter as they advanced.

"John? John, can you hear me?"

The voice was firm, but it felt distant, like a fragment of a memory. John's cracked lips parted, his voice a rasp. "Here," he croaked, barely audible.

The closest figure knelt beside him, their gloved hand gripping his arm. The touch was firm, grounding. "We've got him," the voice said, this time directed elsewhere. The hand lifted him slightly, and John's body protested, every nerve aflame.

"I… I'm John," he stammered, his words slurred. "What… what is happening?"

The figure hesitated, their masked face tilting slightly. "You're safe now. We're extracting you."

Safe? The word felt like a cruel joke. John let out a broken laugh that turned into a sob. "My family," he whispered, his voice cracking. "My son. Is he alive? Did he make it?"

Another figure approached, their voice distinctly female. It carried a weight that chilled John to his core. "We… found him," she said carefully. "But…"

John's blood ran cold. "But what?" he demanded, his voice rising. "Tell me! What happened to my son?"

The first figure removed his helmet, revealing a weathered face etched with lines of sorrow. His eyes met John's, and the weight in them made John's stomach churn. "You don't want to see this," he said softly.

"I need to see it," John roared, his voice raw. "Show me!"

The man sighed deeply and pressed a finger to his earpiece. "Jennie," he said quietly, "send the images."

The female figure's voice crackled through his comms, hesitant. "Nathan… are you sure?"

"He has a right to know," Nathan replied. "Send them."

A tablet was handed to John, its screen flickering to life. His trembling hands struggled to hold it steady. And then, the image filled the screen.

Lucas. Impaled on a jagged tree. His small body twisted grotesquely, ribs jutting out like shattered glass. His head was gone, a jagged stump where it once had been. Blood soaked the ground beneath him, pooling around the phone that had been his only lifeline.

John's scream tore through the night, raw and guttural. The tablet fell from his hands, splattering into the mud as his body convulsed with sobs.

"I failed him," he whispered, his voice barely audible. "I failed them all."

Nathan knelt beside him, his expression grave. "You didn't fail them, John. You survived. That means something."

John shook his head violently, tears streaming down his face. "I have nothing left! Nothing!"

Nathan's grip on his shoulder tightened. "Then fight for the truth. For justice. Come with us. Let's make this right."

John barely registered the words. His vision blurred, his body limp as they lifted him into the waiting helicopter. The last thing he saw before unconsciousness claimed him was the light from the MZOs, casting long, eerie shadows over the campsite where everything he loved had been destroyed.

Reckoning

Sarah sat motionless in the dimly lit room, her breath shallow and uneven. The weight of what she had just heard pressed down on her chest like an iron vice. She looked at John, then at Nathan, her mind reeling, her voice trembling as she finally broke the suffocating silence.

"You were there?" she asked, her eyes wide, searching Nathan's face for any sign that this was some cruel joke.

Nathan nodded slowly, his expression hardened. "Yes. I was there. I saw the devastation. I saw what it was capable of."

Sarah's hand gripped the edge of the table, her knuckles turning bone-white. "So you're telling me," she began, her voice cracking under the weight of disbelief, "that this thing—this... monster—it's real? And it's out there? Right now?"

John leaned forward, his voice raw and heavy with unrelenting grief. "Sarah, this isn't some horror story. It's real. It's out there, and it can't be stopped."

Her laugh was sharp, almost hysterical. "A werewolf? Are you seriously telling me there's a goddamn werewolf loose in the reserve?" She shook her head, her breaths coming faster, her chest rising and falling as panic clawed its way into her thoughts. "How does no one know about this? How has this been kept a secret?"

Nathan leaned forward, his tone steady and calm, a stark contrast to

Sarah's rising hysteria. "Because we make sure no one knows," he said, his words deliberate and cold. "This isn't the only one out there, but this one... this one is different. It's something we've hunted for centuries."

Sarah's laughter turned bitter, biting. "Centuries? What are you, some kind of holy order?" she spat, her tone dripping with disbelief.

John's head shook slowly, his voice tinged with exhaustion. "Not quite," he muttered. "But they know what they're doing. They've saved thousands of lives over the years."

Nathan's gaze didn't falter, his piercing eyes locking with Sarah's. "We're called Phantome," he said, his voice void of any hesitation. "We don't exist in the eyes of society. We've given up everything—our identities, our lives—to make sure people like you can live without knowing what's really out there. Without living in fear."

Sarah's voice faltered, the fire in her defiance dimming. "And John? What about him?"

Nathan's jaw tightened, his voice heavy. "John's family was destroyed because of this thing. But he survived. He's a witness to what we've been fighting."

Sarah turned to John, her eyes glistening with tears. "I... I don't even know what to say. I'm so sorry. I had no idea—"

John's face twisted with grief and unrelenting anger. "Don't be sorry for me, Sarah," he growled, his voice barely above a whisper. "Be sorry for them. Be sorry for Erika, for Lucas, for my wife. They were everything to me. And now they're gone."

The raw, unfiltered anguish in his voice cut through Sarah like a knife. She reached for him instinctively, but he flinched away, his body coiled tight with rage.

"Sarah," Nathan said gently, redirecting her attention. "This creature we're dealing with—it's unique. The only one of its kind. And for some reason, it's following you."

Sarah froze. "What do you mean, following me?" she whispered, her voice trembling, the weight of the implication suffocating.

Nathan's expression softened, but his words were like a punch to the gut. "We've been tracking it. Every time it surfaces, it's near places where you've been."

"That's... that's impossible," she stammered, shaking her head. "Why would it be following me?"

"That's what we need to figure out," Nathan said. "But you need to understand—this isn't some mindless animal. It's intelligent. Strategic. We've shot it, blown it up, set traps, and nothing works. It survives. Every. Single. Time."

Sarah's hands trembled as she pressed them against her mouth, her mind racing with the horror of it all. "You've been hunting it for centuries, and nothing works? How do you expect to stop it now?"

Nathan's silence was deafening. "We don't stop it," he admitted, his voice heavy. "We manage it. Contain it. Limit the damage."

Sarah's laughter was hollow, bitter. "Limit the damage?" she repeated, her voice rising. "That's what you call what happened to John's family? Limiting the damage?"

Nathan's face darkened. "We did everything we could, Sarah. But this one... it's different. It's faster, stronger, smarter. And now it's personal."

Sarah's breath hitched. "Personal?"

John's voice cut through the tension like a blade, low and filled with venom. "It took everything from me," he growled. "And now it's coming for you."

The room fell into a suffocating silence. Sarah's chest tightened as the reality of their words crushed down on her. She looked down at the sketchbook in her lap, the crude lines of the creature she had drawn staring back at her. It wasn't just a figment of her imagination anymore. It was real. It was out there.

Tears blurred her vision. "Why me?" she whispered, her voice cracking. "Why is it after me?"

Nathan placed a hand on her shoulder, his voice softer now. "We don't know yet," he said. "But we're going to find out. And we're going to keep you safe."

Sarah looked up at him, her eyes brimming with fear and defiance. "You better," she said, her voice shaking. "Because if it finds me, I won't survive what John did. I can't... I can't go through that."

Nathan's gaze didn't waver, but his grip on her shoulder tightened slightly. "You're stronger than you think," he said. "And you're not alone in this. Not anymore."

John's eyes remained fixed on the floor, his fists clenched so tightly his knuckles turned white. "She needs to know the truth," he muttered, his voice barely audible but laced with anger. "All of it."

Nathan hesitated, his jaw tightening before he finally nodded. "Soon," he promised, his voice firm. "But right now, we need to focus on keeping her alive."

The weight of their words settled over the room like a storm cloud, suffocating and inescapable. Sarah's world had been shattered, her understanding of reality ripped apart. And yet, deep down, she knew they were right.

The only way to survive was to face the darkness head-on. But for the first time in her life, Sarah wasn't sure she was strong enough to do it.

Gatekeeper

Inside the gatehouse, the warden leaned back in his chair, his phone pressed lazily against his ear as he engaged in idle conversation. The dim light from the overhead bulb cast long shadows across the room, barely keeping the encroaching darkness at bay. The faint buzz of the monitors displaying the security feed was a constant backdrop—a hum that assured him everything was in order.

Then, without warning, the screens flickered.

The warden paused mid-sentence, his eyes narrowing as he turned toward the monitors. Static replaced the steady image of the external cameras. A faint buzz, and then darkness. The main feed cut out completely, leaving the screens blank.

"Damn it," he muttered, hanging up the phone. He tapped one of the monitors with a finger, but it remained unresponsive. His hand hovered over the desk, instinctively reaching for the radio. "Gatehouse to Central. We've got a camera and lighting failure at the perimeter. Could be a system glitch. I'm stepping out to take a look."

The radio crackled to life. "Copy that, Gatehouse. Report back ASAP."

The warden grabbed his flashlight, the weight of it suddenly feeling insufficient. The faint unease that pricked at the back of his mind was easy to dismiss at first—an overreaction, he told himself. But as he stepped outside, the atmosphere shifted.

The floodlights lining the perimeter were extinguished, leaving the path shrouded in darkness. The air was heavy, unnaturally still. His boots crunched against the gravel as he approached the towering steel gate. It loomed ahead, a barrier meant to shield the hospital's grounds from the outside world. But in the absence of light, it looked more like a tomb.

As he reached for the side gate's small control panel, the buzz of the gate's intercom filled the silence.

The warden froze.

The sound hadn't come from his actions. It was deliberate—a signal from the outside.

His heart thudded against his ribs as he pressed the button to respond. "Hello? Identify yourself!"

No answer.

He glanced at the perimeter camera mounted near the gate, his flashlight beam catching the severed wires dangling freely.

"Hello?" he tried again, louder this time. "Who's there?"

The air remained silent, oppressive, as if the darkness itself was holding its breath. Swallowing hard, he moved to unlock the smaller access door built into the gate. The hinges groaned as it swung open, revealing the world beyond—a stretch of gravel that dissolved into the black abyss of the surrounding forest.

The warden stepped through, his flashlight slicing through the dark. Shadows danced and twisted at the edge of the beam, the skeletal outlines of trees swaying in the faint breeze.

"What the hell is going on…" he murmured, his voice barely above a whisper.

Then he heard it.

A low, guttural rumble.

The sound was faint at first, like a distant growl carried on the wind. But it grew louder, deeper, until it vibrated through the ground beneath him. A sick, warm breath brushed the back of his neck, carrying the stench of decay and wet fur.

His blood turned to ice.

He turned slowly, every muscle in his body locking in terror. The flashlight trembled in his hand as the beam caught the faint outline of something massive. Two glowing red eyes blinked into existence, their crimson light piercing through the dark.

The warden stumbled back, his breath hitching. His hand flew to the pistol holstered at his hip, but before he could draw it, the creature lunged.

A force like a freight train slammed into him, knocking him off his feet. The flashlight flew from his grip, spinning wildly as its beam illuminated the chaos—clawed hands gripping him, teeth glinting in the brief light.

He hit the ground hard, the air forced from his lungs as pain exploded through his chest. The creature's weight bore down on him, claws digging into his flesh as it dragged him toward the tree line.

He tried to scream, but the sound was choked off as a clawed hand clamped around his throat. His body thrashed against the crushing grip, his boots scraping against the gravel as he was pulled into the shadows.

Gunfire erupted from the gatehouse—a frantic volley of three sharp bursts that shattered the silence. The creature didn't flinch.

The warden's world spun as he was hoisted into the air, the ground falling away beneath him. The creature's red eyes burned into his as it growled—a deep, guttural sound that resonated with pure malice.

A final scream tore from the warden's throat, echoing into the night.

And then, silence.

The forest swallowed the sound as quickly as it had swallowed the man. The gatehouse lights flickered back to life, their cold glow illuminating the abandoned flashlight lying in the gravel.

But the warden was gone.

Sacrifice and Escape

A nearby patrol heard the shots and ran toward the gate, their flashlights bouncing wildly with each step. When they arrived, the small door hung ajar, swinging lazily on its hinges. The flashlight the warden had carried lay abandoned in the gravel, smeared with blood. One soldier shone his beam toward the ground and stopped cold.

Massive tracks, too large to belong to any wolf, led away from the gate. The prints were smeared with crimson, trailing toward the main building.

"Jesus Christ," one soldier whispered, his voice barely audible. "What the hell is this?"

Another soldier bolted to the gatehouse, slamming his hand against the emergency alarm button. A deafening klaxon blared across the compound, cutting through the stillness like a blade. Soldiers scrambled to their posts, their radios crackling with frantic orders.

The lights flickered back on, casting long, jagged shadows against the trees, but the forest beyond remained a wall of impenetrable darkness. Somewhere within that darkness, something moved. Something big. Something unstoppable.

And it was coming for them.

Sarah sat motionless in the dimly lit room, her breath shallow and uneven. The distant klaxon screamed, an eerie counterpoint to the tension choking the air inside. Nathan stood abruptly, his body tense, his gaze fixed out the window. Something was wrong. The hairs on the back of Sarah's neck stood on end.

"Nathan… what's going on?" Her voice was small, a tremor betraying her fear.

Nathan didn't answer immediately. Instead, he shot a look at John, whose face fell into a grim mask. Without hesitation, John pushed himself up, wincing as he moved to the other window.

Sarah opened her mouth to question again, but then she heard it too—the distant pop-pop-pop of automatic gunfire. Small. Muffled. Like firecrackers far off. But then came something else. Screams. The kind that made her stomach twist.

Nathan pulled a small black phone from his pocket, clipped an earpiece to his ear, and turned his back on them. His posture was rigid, every muscle taut.

Sarah turned to John, her voice cracking. "John… what is that? What's happening?"

John didn't answer immediately. He just looked at her, his face pale but resigned. "We'll know soon enough."

Nathan's voice was sharp as he barked into the earpiece. "Jennie, report!"

Jennie's voice crackled faintly. "It's inside, Nathan. The perimeter's compromised. You need to get out now!"

Nathan's jaw clenched. "How long before you're here?"

"Fifteen minutes, tops. I'm activating Project Alpha. You need to move."

Sarah blinked, her breath catching. Project Alpha. She knew that name. From where? Her mind raced, but the answer wouldn't come.

"Fifteen minutes?" Nathan muttered under his breath, swearing softly. He turned toward them, his face set in stone. "We don't have much time."

"Project Alpha?" Sarah stammered, looking between them. "What the hell is that?"

Nathan grabbed her by the arm, not roughly, but with enough force to snap her back to the present. "Move, Sarah. Now."

"Where are we going?"

Nathan didn't answer as he cracked open the door and peeked into the hallway. The emergency lights bathed everything in a deep, crimson red. It felt like they were standing inside a beating heart.

The gunfire outside was closer now. Sporadic bursts mixed with something else—something worse. A wet, heavy sound. A deep growl that seemed to reverberate through the very walls.

“This way,” Nathan whispered urgently, pulling her forward. John trailed close behind, his fists clenched at his sides, his knuckles white from tension.

The hallway stretched before them, the flickering red light dancing like flames. Sarah’s legs trembled beneath her. She didn’t know if it was the adrenaline or sheer terror keeping her upright. She glanced over at the security locker Nathan had shown her earlier. Now, instead of a keypad, it glowed with the word: ACCESS GRANTED.

Nathan pressed his phone against the lock, and it clicked. The door slid open silently, revealing its contents—gear unlike anything Sarah had ever seen. Weapons gleamed under the soft interior lights. Ammunition. Body armor. Devices she couldn’t name.

Nathan didn’t waste time. He grabbed a massive shotgun, its barrel thick and menacing, and tossed it to John. “You know how to use this?”

John caught it awkwardly, his face dark. “Do I have a choice?”

Nathan barely glanced at him. “No.”

Sarah stared at the cache, her heart pounding in her ears. “What about me? Do I get a weapon?”

Nathan turned to her, his gaze steady. “No. You don’t want this thing to see you as a threat.”

“What?” she stammered, her voice rising. “You’re kidding, right?”

Nathan ignored her protests, his attention snapping to the far end of the hallway as a low, dragging sound echoed toward them. It was faint but unmistakable—the sound of claws scraping against the tile.

It's inside.

Nathan's grip on his weapon tightened. He checked his phone again. "Ten minutes," he muttered.

"We need to get to the stairs or the elevator," he whispered. "Now."

John nodded silently, his knuckles white around the shotgun.

They moved quickly, staying close to the wall. Sarah's breath came in short, shaky bursts. She couldn't stop looking over her shoulder, half-expecting to see glowing red eyes peering back at her through the shadows.

A sudden bang shattered the silence. The main door at the far end of the hall exploded open, slamming into the wall so hard it cracked the plaster. Sarah's scream caught in her throat as Nathan shoved her into a nearby room, John diving into the room across from them.

For a moment, everything went still.

Then came the sound.

The slow, deliberate scrape… scrape… scrape of claws on linoleum. Each step echoed, louder and closer. Sarah pressed her back against the wall, covering her mouth to stifle a sob. She could hear the creature breathing—low and rhythmic, like a beast savoring the hunt.

Nathan held a finger to his lips, signaling her to stay silent. Sweat dripped down his temple, but his face was pure focus.

Sarah squeezed her eyes shut, praying it would pass them by.

The scratching stopped.

Silence.

Nathan's phone vibrated faintly. He glanced at it, then back to Sarah. Eight minutes.

A sudden growl rumbled from the hallway, deep and bone-chilling. The creature exhaled sharply, the sound almost human. Sarah froze. It knows we're here.

Nathan met her eyes, his voice barely a whisper. "We move on my signal. Ready yourself."

Sarah nodded shakily, her fingers trembling as she gripped her knees.

And then—

A loud crash shattered the stillness as the door across the hall was ripped from its hinges. John's voice bellowed, "Run!"

Final

They bolted from the room as the hallway erupted into chaos. Behind them, John's shotgun roared, the deafening blasts ripping through the corridors like thunderclaps. Each shot reverberated, shaking the walls, a desperate, defiant symphony against the encroaching nightmare. Sarah stumbled, her feet slipping on something slick, her breaths sharp and uneven. Nathan didn't let her falter. He yanked her forward, his grip an iron vice around her arm.

"Keep moving!" Nathan barked, his voice raw, fierce—a leader in the face of doom. "He's holding it off! Don't let his effort be in vain!"

The hallway pulsed with crimson light from flickering emergency strobes. Each harsh flash turned the cracked walls and shattered tiles into a grotesque, shifting nightmare of shadows. Blood glistened across the floor, dark pools mingling with debris. The air was thick, suffocating—scorched metal, sweat, and something darker still. Something rancid and ancient, like a predator's breath against the back of your neck.

Then—

Click.

The metallic sound sliced through the chaos like a knife. John's shotgun had fallen silent.

Sarah froze mid-step. Her heart seized, her chest constricting as if icy claws had wrapped around her lungs. She turned her head, her voice a broken whisper. “No… no, no, no.”

A low growl rolled from the darkness, rumbling like an earthquake. It was mocking—deliberate. The steady scrape of claws against tile followed, each step a metronome counting down John’s final moments.

Nathan spun on his heel, his rifle raised. “Move, Sarah!” he hissed, but she couldn’t. Her body was paralyzed, pinned by the primal dread that bled from the shadows.

And then the beast emerged.

It stepped into the stuttering light, a towering wall of sinew and shadow. Its red eyes burned, pools of molten hate that locked onto John. The shotgun dangled useless in his grip, his knuckles white against the barrel. Blood dripped from the creature’s maw, splashing onto the tiles with a sickening hiss. Its breath curled outward—hot, rancid, and alive—like a poison fog spreading its corruption.

Nathan’s voice cut through the dread. “Duck, John!”

John dropped instinctively, and Nathan fired. The rifle barked like a cannon, the recoil slamming into his shoulder. Two rounds hit their mark, punching into the beast’s flank with meaty thuds.

The creature roared—thick, guttural, and monstrous—as it crashed into the wall, dust and plaster raining down.

“It worked!” John gasped, spinning toward Nathan, hope flickering in his bloodshot eyes.

The beast moved. Faster than thought, faster than anything so massive had any right to be. Its claw lashed out and closed around John's ankle like a steel trap.

"No!" Nathan bellowed.

John's scream was sharp, raw—a sound that scraped against the soul. His nails clawed at the tiles, leaving red-streaked gouges as the beast dragged him backward into the dark.

"John!" Nathan surged forward.

The door to the side room slammed shut, rattling the walls like a thunderclap.

Inside the room, the world turned into a living nightmare. The creature threw John across the room with inhuman force, his body crashing into a metal cabinet. Pain erupted through his ribs, sharp and all-consuming. Blood trickled from his mouth as he staggered to his feet, his defiance unwavering despite the agony.

The beast stepped closer, its eyes gleaming with malicious delight. Its claws dripped with blood, each step deliberate, savoring the moment.

"What are you waiting for?" John spat, his voice hoarse but filled with venom. "You've already taken everything from me. My wife. My kids. What's left, you bastard? Come on! Take it!"

The creature tilted its head, its grotesque snout curling into what could only be described as a sneer. Its claws flexed, the tips scraping against the tiles with a sound that set John's teeth on edge.

"You're nothing but a fucking coward," John growled, his voice breaking but defiant. "An overgrown mutt hiding in the shadows."

With a guttural snarl, the beast lunged. John dodged to the side, grabbing a metal pipe from the wreckage around him. He swung with all his strength, the pipe connecting with the creature's jaw. The impact echoed through the room, but the beast barely flinched. Instead, it smiled—a horrifying, toothy grin that chilled John to his core.

It swiped at him, claws raking across his chest. The pain was blinding, the force sending him sprawling to the floor. Blood pooled beneath him as the beast loomed over him, its breath hot and putrid against his face.

John's vision blurred, but he forced himself to look up. His lips curled into a weak smile, blood staining his teeth. "You think this is the end?" he rasped, his voice barely audible. "Fuck you."

With the last of his strength, he spat a mouthful of blood into the creature's face. The beast recoiled slightly, its growl reverberating through the walls. John laughed, a broken, bitter sound that echoed in the silence.

The creature's claws plunged into his abdomen, twisting cruelly. John arched, his cry strangled as the creature tore into him. But even as darkness claimed him, there was no fear—only love. Images of his family filled his vision—Erika's laughter as she danced in the sunlight,

Lucas's stubborn, determined gaze, his wife's warm touch against his cheek. He clung to those fragments, refusing to let the beast win.

"I'll see you soon," he whispered, more to himself than the creature.

The beast snarled, its claws ripping through flesh and bone as it finished him. Blood splattered across the walls, the sickening sound of tearing meat filling the room. And then, silence.

Down the hallway, Sarah's broken sobs echoed faintly, a sound so full of grief it felt like the walls themselves mourned. Nathan grabbed her arm and yanked her toward the stairwell, his face carved from stone, though his jaw trembled.

John's final scream—raw, guttural, and human—ripped through the air, then silence.

Nathan's voice was soft, hollow as he spoke. "He's gone," he whispered, each word shattering him. "Move."

The stairwell door was locked. Nathan fired, shattering the lock. The elevator dinged beside them as Jennie stepped out, her rifle already aimed. "Move!" she barked.

The beast's roar erupted behind them, and it barreled out of the room, blood dripping from its claws. Jennie hurled two metallic discs. They hit the floor, expanding into electrified nets that crackled with blue energy. The beast lunged, caught mid-air, its growls vibrating through the walls as it thrashed against the restraints.

"Go!" Nathan shoved Sarah into the elevator, diving in just as Jennie slid inside. The doors snapped shut as the creature's roar tore through the space, primal and furious. The elevator ascended, the air thick with silence except for Sarah's quiet, broken whisper.

"We left him. We left him to die."

Nathan placed a trembling hand on her shoulder. His voice was rough, barely steady. "He made sure you lived. Don't waste it."

The rooftop doors opened, and the thrum of helicopter blades greeted them. Nathan pulled Sarah toward the chopper while Jennie covered their retreat. The beast erupted onto the rooftop just as the helicopter began to lift off, its claws swiping through the air, nearly grazing the fuselage. Nathan yanked Jennie inside at the last second. The chopper shuddered, a deep gouge carved into its side.

Sarah stared at the creature, still on the platform, its head thrown back in a howl—a sound that carried across the night, vibrating in their bones.

"What… what is happening? Who are you guys?!" she whispered.

Jennie's face was unreadable as she turned to her. "Welcome aboard."

Nathan met Sarah's gaze, his voice low, resigned. "We're Phantome."

Two Weeks Later

The quiet suburban neighborhood lay cloaked in darkness. An unnatural stillness hung in the air, heavy and suffocating, as though the world itself was holding its breath. Streetlights flickered feebly, their dull glow barely pushing back the shadows that seemed to creep closer, alive and hungry.

Inside one of the houses, a soft hum from the television broke the silence. Six-year-old Emily sat cross-legged on the living room floor, surrounded by forgotten toys. Dolls, stuffed animals, and building blocks lay strewn about her like discarded friends. The TV flickered erratically, casting blinking shadows across the room as a news anchor's voice droned in the background.

"Residents are urged to stay indoors. A state of emergency remains in effect. Lock all doors and windows. Do not—"

The signal crackled, cutting off mid-sentence. Static hissed across the screen for a heartbeat before the anchor's voice returned, distorted now, as if coming from underwater.

"Do not let anyone inside."

Emily barely registered the warning. Grown-up words. They didn't matter to her. Her mom and dad were upstairs—she could hear the faint hum of their voices muffled through the ceiling. They were busy, too busy to play.

Her small hands fiddled absently with her dolls, but loneliness gnawed at her chest. She sighed, casting a glance toward the window, where darkness pressed against the glass like a silent intruder.

Tap. Tap.

A sound—soft, like fingertips against glass.

Emily's head snapped up. She looked around, confused. The TV buzzed softly, the static creeping into her ears like whispers.

The tapping came again.

Tap. Tap. Tap.

This time sharper, like nails raking delicately against the windowpane. She turned toward the sound, her heart fluttering as a chill crawled up her spine. The living room, dimly lit by the flickering screen, suddenly seemed vast, the corners stretching into endless darkness.

Emily stood, her bare feet silent on the carpet as she crept to the sofa. She climbed up, pressing her small hands against the windowsill, her breath fogging the glass.

Two red eyes stared back at her.

They burned like embers—cold and deliberate, yet filled with something… familiar.

Emily's lips parted, her voice a faint whisper. "...Hello?"

The figure outside didn't move, but the eyes blinked slowly, unnervingly human in their gesture. Its shape, barely visible in the gloom, was massive—a dark silhouette with hunched shoulders and something like fur, but wrong. Its limbs seemed too long, its shape shifting in the shadows as though it didn't quite belong.

Her small voice broke the silence again. "Are you lost? Do you need help?"

The creature tilted its head—slowly, unnaturally—as if it understood her words.

"Emily!"

Her mother's voice rang from upstairs, sharp and distant. "Bedtime soon, honey!"

Emily glanced toward the ceiling, then back to the window. The creature hadn't moved. It stared at her, its red eyes boring into her like it could see her thoughts. It looked… sad.

"You look like you need a friend," she said softly, her voice trembling.

The creature raised a clawed hand. It moved with deliberate slowness, the talons glinting faintly in the stuttering light. It pointed—to the front door.

Emily hesitated. A whisper in her mind—a voice that wasn't her own—murmured, Let me in.

Her small face brightened. "Do you want to come inside?"

The creature blinked.

She scrambled off the sofa and padded to the front door, the static from the TV filling the silence like a chorus of whispers. Her small hands fumbled with the lock. The deadbolt clicked, loud in the silence, as she cracked the door open just enough for the cold night air to slither in.

An overwhelming smell hit her—a mix of damp earth, rotting meat, and something sweet, like overripe fruit.

Emily didn't seem to notice. She smiled faintly. "There you go."

Without waiting, she turned and ran upstairs, her footsteps light and cheerful.

In the master bedroom, her parents were busy arguing, their voices too hushed to carry. Emily burst through the door, her face beaming with innocent pride.

"Mommy! Daddy! I made a new friend!"

Her mother turned, frowning. "What do you mean, sweetheart?"

Her father looked up sharply. "Emily… did you open the door?"

Emily nodded, her voice full of excitement. "Yes! He was lonely, so I let him in!"

A sudden cold draft swept through the house. The light in the room dimmed, the air thickening with a pressure that made it hard to breathe.

Emily's father bolted for the door, his voice sharp. "Emily, what did you—"

The shadow came first.

It spilled across the hallway floor, vast and consuming, swallowing the light as it advanced. A low, guttural growl vibrated through the walls, deep and hungry—a sound that dug into bone and marrow.

Emily's father froze, his voice catching in his throat. "What… what is that?"

Her mother screamed as the doorway filled with red eyes—burning, unblinking, watching them with cold amusement. The massive figure stepped forward, its clawed hand scraping against the frame, leaving deep grooves in the wood.

Emily smiled, clutching her mother's hand. "See? I told you. He's my friend."

The room plunged into darkness.

And then the screams began—raw, terrified, and short-lived.

In the hallway, the static hissed louder from the television, like a thousand whispers in the dark.

Somewhere in the night, a single porch light flickered out, leaving the quiet suburban street in total darkness.

End of Book 1

Acknowledgements

Thank you for venturing into the chilling world of *In The Shadows*. Writing this book has been an extraordinary journey, and I am deeply grateful for the support and encouragement I've received along the way.

To my family and friends, your unwavering belief in me has been my anchor throughout this process. To my beta readers, your insights and dedication have been instrumental in shaping this story into what it is today. And to you, the reader, thank you for allowing this tale to take root in your imagination. It's your curiosity that brings these pages to life.

This book is the first in an intense trilogy—a psychological horror thriller with threads of action and suspense woven through every twist and turn. As the story unfolds, the shadows will grow darker, the stakes higher, and the truths more harrowing. The next installment promises to delve deeper into the psychological torment, blending visceral horror with adrenaline-fueled action, creating an experience as thought-provoking as it is nerve-wracking.

Thank you for embarking on this journey with me. Your trust, your time, and your willingness to step into the unknown mean the world to me. Until next time, embrace the suspense, and remember—the shadows always have more to reveal.

Made in the USA
Columbia, SC
24 March 2025

55623948R00159